TOURIST TRAP

A COZY MYSTERY

SHEILA ROBERTS

ROBERTS INK PRESS

ALSO BY SHEILA ROBERTS

For a complete listing of over 50 books by Sheila Roberts, please visit her website: www.sheilasplace.com

Dear Reader,

Many years ago, when I was a sweet young thing, my husband had a side business of conducting small tour groups around Europe. I went along on one of these tours, acting as the social director. I noticed a very strange thing when we were touring a monastery in Austria. The only protection they had for their priceless antiquarian books was chicken wire. Chicken wire? Seriously? Oh, what trusting monks!

Anyway, I thought it would be fun to write a mystery based on this not so secure security system. I'm sure by now the monks have modernized, but, for the sake of the story, let's pretend they haven't.

And, on another note, on our last visit to Germany I'd hoped to get back into the charming grotto at King Ludwig's Linderhof castle and make sure all was as I remembered there. Alas, I was hugely disappointed to learn that it was closed for repairs. Honestly, what's with these people? How dare they close one of my favorite tourist attractions for maintenance?

Ah, well, this is, after all a work of fiction. So set aside your disbelief and come along on the trip with me. It's the one and only mystery I ever wrote. Maybe after reading it, you'll think it *just as well that I went a different direction. Or maybe you'll simply enjoy taking the tour with these crazy characters. That's what I'm hoping. Bon voyage!*

Sheila

P.S. Once upon a time, I did meet a race car driver in a hotel restaurant bar. Maybe fact is stranger than fiction. Or maybe it simply comes in handy when you're writing fiction.

PROLOGUE

Once Upon a Mountain

Gilly Greer leaned on the railing of the scenic overlook and scowled down at the mists curling around the Tegelberg, obscuring the view of the mountainside and valley below. Why had their tour guide bothered to drag them all the way up here?

She turned away and sighed. The only thing they could see was the lodge, the restaurant, and the souvenir stand. Half a dozen people milled around the latter, buying postcards, including the tour group's own Inge Brueckner, the man eater. Next to her stood her current side dish, Ed Robinson, short, balding, and middle-aged. Gilly had seen Clint and Lisa Madsen pass that way a few minutes ago, but now they'd vanished somewhere into the mists.

Gilly's disgruntled gaze strayed to the hang-gliding ramp and the man stretched out on the platform end of it, waiting for clear sky. "Why are we here?" she grumped.

"Is that one of those deep philosophical questions?" asked her companion.

"Seriously. Why on earth did Rob bring us here? We can't see a thing."

"He probably thought it would burn off by the time we got up here," said Royce Clark.

"But why not go to the castles first?" Gilly persisted.

Royce shrugged. "This was on the way to the castles."

Gilly shook her head. "What a waste of time."

"Nah, it ain't a waste. Here." He whipped out his cell phone and backed up a few feet. "Pose pretty and let me take your picture." She smiled self-consciously for him and tried to strike a casual pose.

"Hallo Schatzi."

"Now, why'd you go and do that?" he complained as Gilly frowned.

Inge just had that effect on women. "Hi Inge," Gilly said in less than enthusiastic tones as the tall, busty brunette sidled up to Royce. As usual, she had her selfie stick in hand.

"Where's Ed?" Gilly would have liked to add, *the man you finally settled on. Remember him?*

In all fairness to Inge, Gilly had to admit it was hard to remember lesser men when standing next to Royce Clark, six feet of well-muscled male with dark hair, strong chin, and screen test worthy brown eyes. He was certainly the most gorgeous thing Gilly had ever seen.

Inge shrugged. "He disappeared. One minute he was with me at the souvenir stand, the next he was gone."

"Why don't you go look for him?" Gilly suggested sweetly. "He can't have gone too far."

Just then a man's scream drifted up to them from somewhere beyond the hang gliders' ramp.

"What was that?" asked Inge, and clutched Royce's arm.

"It came from that direction," he said, and after prying her fingers loose, ran off toward the ramp. The women followed him, and they reached it to find the hang glider and some other German tourists, talking in hushed tones and peering down into the amorphous, white swirl.

"What happened?" called their fellow tour group member Ida Thompson, huffing up behind them. Ida Thompson had said good-bye to middle-age and was a bit on the plump side, a combination that guaranteed some huffing.

"We heard a scream," Gilly told her. "It sounded like it came from this direction."

"Help!" cried a male voice.

Everyone looked to the path which sloped down past the ramp, leading to another lookout point. Gilly's mouth dropped as David Schwartz, the group's enfant terrible, staggered up the path to them, one hand holding his side, the other arm pointing back in the direction he had come.

"Down there," he panted. "A man just fell off the mountain!"

"What?" gasped the others.

"A man just fell off the mountain. I saw him." With a groan, he collapsed on the ground and put his head in his hands.

"You poor boy," said Ida. She patted his shoulder with a pudgy hand. "You've had a terrible shock. Did you see how it happened?"

"No. I only saw this body hang gliding without the glider. My God, I'm going to have nightmares for the rest of my life," he predicted. "I think I'm gonna hurl."

"Let's get you someplace where you can sit down and have a glass of water," Ida said. Fussing and clucking, she led him away.

"We better report this," said Royce.

Just then Carl Marks, another one of their group members

came into sight, strolling leisurely up the same path David had taken. "Carl, have you seen Rob?" called Royce.

Carl shook his head. "What's the matter?" he asked, joining them.

"Somebody just took a dive off the mountain," Royce informed him. "And it looks like David may be the only one who witnessed it. Let's see if we can find Rob. I'll go that way. Carl, you check over there. You girls go that-a-way."

The two women didn't find their leader, but they did run into Clint and Lisa. "What's going on?" asked Clint. "We thought we heard somebody scream."

"A man fell off the mountain," chorused Gilly and Inge.

Clint's mouth dropped. "Did anybody see it happen?" asked his wife.

"David saw him go over," said Gilly.

"Where is David?" asked Lisa, looking around.

"Ida took him to the restaurant for a drink of water," said Gilly.

"He'll need more than that," said Clint. "Come to think of it, I could use a beer."

"Good idea," agreed Inge and they all went to the restaurant, leaving Royce and Carl to find their leader.

A few minutes later the two men joined them, along with Rob Warsaw, their tour guide, and the owner of Budget Adventures. Rob had informed the manager of the restaurant, who had put in a call to the police. There was nothing to do but wait and participate vicariously in David's hair-raising adventure while he retold his tale.

"You were around there, Carl. You didn't see anything?" Rob asked after David had finished.

Carl shook his head. "I'm afraid not."

"I wonder if we'll be able to see the body when this fog lifts," said Inge.

Gilly blanched at the thought and took a restorative gulp of her beer.

The group was on their second round of drinks and Ida was wondering what possible help they could be to the police when the men in question showed up, an older one who was wearing what looked like a permanent frown, and a short, younger one. The restaurant manager escorted the two officers over, then stayed, taking a position next to the table where he could see and hear all. Rob rose and greeted them.

"Wer von Ihnen hat den Unfall gemeldet?" asked the shorter policeman. His partner pulled a small notepad and pencil out of his pocket and began to write.

"Ich," said Rob.

"What'd he say?" Royce whispered to Gilly.

"Ich," she whispered back.

"I know that. What did the cop say?"

Gilly shook her head, wishing she could remember more of her high school German. "I'm not sure. I think he's asking who reported the accident."

Rob motioned to David, who slid from behind the table and stood up next to him. "Tell him what you saw," he commanded.

David nodded. "It was horrible. I'd gone down to that lookout below the ramp to take pictures, and next thing I knew I saw this body falling."

Rob interpreted as fast as he could, trying to keep up with David's excited explanation.

David continued, hands fluttering. "I didn't see him go over. In fact, I probably wouldn't have seen him at all, except he screamed."

"Er hat geschrieen," translated Rob.

"Ja," nodded David, his awful accent making Gilly blush. "I don't know where he landed, because it was still foggy down there."

The short policeman said something, and Rob nodded.

"What's he saying?" Royce asked.

Gilly shook her head. "Beats me."

"Sorry," Rob apologized. "We've got to go show the police where David saw the man go over. You all may want to order something to eat. I don't know how long all this is going to take."

It was almost an hour before Rob and David returned. "What's the news?" asked Royce. "Are they gonna let us go?"

Rob nodded. "The fog is finally lifting enough to where you can see the body. As far as the police can tell, David was the only eyewitness. But they've got a copy of our itinerary and our addresses so they're letting us leave."

"Wouldn't you know, now that it's clearing up, we're leaving," said Inge as they crowded into the cable car to go back down the mountain.

Gilly shook her head fatalistically. It figured.

The way this tour was going, nothing would surprise her. There had been a lot of goofy things happening.

Were they connected? Like scattered beads, she began to mentally pick up past events and string them together....

ONE

Gilly arrived at the Seattle-Tacoma International Airport at six p.m., armed with a Starbucks frap to fight off the mid-July heat and ready for romance and adventure, her suitcase full of new outfits (not to mention new lingerie).

On his website, Rob Warsaw had promised her London, Amsterdam, Bavaria, and even Vienna, all for a bargain. Of course, he hadn't promised the romance or adventure. Gilly had assumed that since she was paying all this money and going to foreign countries that those would be thrown in as a bonus.

She didn't need much, really. Anything was more romantic than the drudgery of single parenthood and running a house-cleaning business.

She'd already met most of her travelling companions at a get-acquainted dinner at the Schnitzelbank restaurant, but she refused to admit what she was beginning to suspect, that romance would probably not be present on this trip. Or adventure. How much adventure could you have traipsing around with a bunch of other Americans? Especially these. It served her right. This was what came of watching too many rom-coms and adventure movies.

She obviously hadn't thought things through, especially when she'd further deprived herself of any romance by checking the space next to "Willing to share a room." By doing so she'd save a lot of money, but at what cost? There would be no sitting on the bed enjoying German chocolate and kisses with a third-party present.

Well, a girl could still manage romance on a river cruise or walking along a quaint cobbled street in some German town. That, however, was possible only if you had someone to be romantic with.

Clint Madsen was nice looking, a man in his late thirties with sun-bleached blonde hair, a mustache, and a great collection of muscles. He also had a pretty, blonde wife named Lisa.

Then there was David Schwartz, a friendly, talkative metrosexual in his early twenties. Too young.

Carl Marks was a Teutonic looking male, hovering close to fifty – a very prime, well- conditioned fifty, complete with firm abdomen and tanned skin. But judging from his sober demeanor and Sphinx-like quiet, he was no love connection, either.

She still remembered her introduction to Carl Baby. "Carl Marks," he'd said brusquely. She'd smiled. Carl had mimicked it by forcing his lips into the world's smallest smile and a certain song about party poopers had come to mind.

Then there'd been Ivan and Ida, the Thompsons. Retired. Ivan was thin and balding and had worn a look of simple innocence all night. His wife was plump, with graying blonde hair, blue eyes, and a freckled snub nose, interested in everyone and assuring one and all that she traveled prepared. Anything anyone needed, whether it be aspirin or mosquito repellant, they could come to her. Everybody's mom.

The only decent available male at the dinner had been Rob Warsaw, their tour guide. He was cute with a baby face, blond hair, and a moustache, somewhere in his middle thirties, which put him right around Gilly's age. But beyond going over their itinerary, he wasn't much of a talker. A little on the shy side. Miss Brueckner would have him for breakfast their first day out.

Gilly knew a man-eater when she saw one, and Ms. Brueckner ("Call me Inge, Schatzi"), from the look of the telltale skin on her neck, had reached an especially hungry age. Inge was tall and leggy with Barbie doll sized boobs that she showcased with a lowcut top, eyelash extensions and collagen enhanced lips, and Gilly knew no little auburn-haired thing could compete with that.

Well, there were still two single mystery men left to meet: Ed Robinson and Royce Clark. Maybe one of them? Hope didn't exactly spring, but it still bubbled a little.

As Gilly took her place at the end of a long line of travelers at airport security, she caught sight of Inge further toward the front. She'd poured herself into a pair of jeans and wore a knit top similar to the one Gilly had on, only on Inge the fabric was considerably more stretched. She was talking to a short, balding, middle-aged man, who was hanging on her every word.

That had to be Ed Robinson. Gilly sighed and wondered why she'd wasted so much money on clothes.

Well, there was still Rob. Maybe he didn't have a woman in his life. Maybe, he could be brought to talk about more than castles and currency values.

And Royce Clark. He'd had some kind of conference come up he had to attend and couldn't fly out with everyone, but he was catching up with them in Amsterdam.

She'd just finished going through security when David Schwartz came up to her, gorgeous in jeans with a white shirt and a slim fit gray blazer and bright blue throwback sneakers. He was the picture of youthful energy, all scrubbed and clean and excited. He wasn't a bad looking kid, thought Gilly in a detached, older sister sort of way. The body was slim and toned, and although his eyes were a little too close set, he did have a nicely shaped nose and a strong jaw line. She wondered if he had a girlfriend.

David unshouldered his bucket bag. "I'm so excited!" he gushed. "Can you believe this is really happening? Oh, there's our fearless leader, the professor. Did you know he teaches high school German?"

"No, I didn't," Gilly said.

Like Ida, David obviously was into knowing all about people. "I guess he just does this as a summer job. Well, I'm going to go tell him I'm here," David concluded and minced off.

Maybe not into girls.

Gilly was halfway to her gate when she ran into Clint Madsen. "We're all killing time in the bar," he told her. "Want to join us?"

"Sure," she said. "As soon as I make a phone call."

As he walked back to the bar, she pulled her cell phone from her purse and called her neighbor, Janet, who was watching her daughter for the first week Gilly was gone.

"Are you having a glamorous time yet?" Janet asked.

"I'm just about to go have a drink in the bar. Does that count?"

"Of course, it counts. When was the last time you had a drink in a bar?"

"The day I got my divorce papers. And you should know. You were with me."

Janet snickered. "Well, then, things are already looking up. Did you meet the new man?"

"Oh, yes. He's short, fat, and bald."

"Hmm," said Janet.

"I should have stayed home and redone the kitchen floor."

"You can redo your kitchen floor any time," said Janet. "You need some fun. Anyway, didn't you say there's still one more man coming? You haven't met him, yet. Right?"

"No, and I can hardly wait. Not."

"All right, so maybe you won't meet the man of your dreams. I'm still predicting you'll have a great time, and I don't expect to see your name come up on my phone any time in the next two weeks. Unless you meet someone fabulous. Then I expect to hear instantly. "I am going to miss you, you know. Nobody else will stay up with me until two a.m. on a Friday night, binging on old episodes of *Friends*. By the way, your daughter's missing you so much she had to console herself by walking with Jess to the Seven-Eleven for a Slurpy."

Gilly felt oddly deflated. Gone only a couple of hours and Mandy had already forgotten her.

"We did have a moment of silence in your honor before the girls left though," Janet added.

"Gee, thanks."

"What can I say? Doug Ball is working there, and if you were a thirteen-year-old girl and you had to pick between going to flirt with a cute fifteen-year-old boy and hanging around with your best friend's thirty-something mom, which would you choose?"

"You're right," said Gilly.

She still took a moment to text an I-love-you to Mandy after saying good-bye to Janet. Happily, Mandy texted an I-love-you back – a great way to begin her trip.

A self-indulgent trip, really. Going off for two weeks and leaving her daughter behind. Except her ex was taking Mandy camping the next week, and she'd informed her mom that hanging out with her cousins and river rafting was way better than traveling with a bunch of boring grown-ups. Boring grown-ups. Who'd have known Mandy was psychic?

The other members of their group, including Ed Robinson, the newest one, were already packed in around a table when Gilly got to the bar. Rob introduced him to Gilly, and he sucked in his stomach and grinned at her.

"Good," Clint said as the waitress appeared. "My beer is here. Man, I can hardly wait to get to Germany and taste that German beer." He elbowed David. "And those German Fräuleins, eh?

Ed laughed appreciatively, and David merely smiled.

"You do like girls, don't you?" teased Clint.

David assured him that he liked girls. "Especially married ones," he concluded, leaning close to Lisa, and smiling at her. Clint didn't appear to see the humor in that remark.

"Where are the Thompsons?" asked Gilly.

"They wanted to get some magazines," Clint told her. "They don't drink," he added and shook his head in bewilderment over such a lifestyle choice.

Gilly turned to Ed. "What do you do for a living, Mr. Robinson?"

"Call me Ed," he said, leering at her.

"Ed," Gilly repeated, and leaned back in her chair, trying to subtly place herself out of grabbing distance.

"I'm pretty much retired," he said.

"You look too young to be retired," Gilly observed, amazed.

Ed was obviously pleased with her remark. "Oh, I could work if I wanted, but I prefer to dabble in investments, let my money work instead. Invested in Apple at the right time."

Clint Madsen let out a low whistle. "I guess you did okay for yourself."

You can say that again, thought Gilly, looking at the large diamond dinner ring on his finger and the Rolex on his wrist.

"Yep." Ed took a satisfied swig from his glass. "I did alright."

Inge smiled at him and said she wished she had a head for business. "But we artists..." she finished, leaving the sentence for her companions to fill in as they wished.

"You're an artist?" David asked excitedly. "What kind of stuff do you do? Impressionist? Post Impressionism? Pop Art?"

"Seascapes," Inge said, and David looked disappointed.

"How can you make a living selling Seascapes?" Clint asked. "I mean, no offense or anything, but it doesn't seem like the kind of thing you can make a lot of money doing."

Inge squirmed. "Most artists aren't appreciated in their own lifetime. I also work as a hostess at Thirteen Coins. But my art is my life," she declared.

Time passed pleasantly as the group chatted, looking for common interests and views. Before their time in the bar was over Gilly felt she had pretty much sized up her companions.

Clint Madsen was a car salesman, and he had the kind of gregarious personality she expected such a person to have. He anticipated having a wonderful time and said he'd cheerfully go along to see any castles and cathedrals that came their way as long as he was kept supplied with plenty of Schnitzel and beer.

His wife, Lisa, was a dental assistant. She appeared equally easy to get along with. Not as talkative as her husband, she still managed to get in a word when she really wanted to, and while Clint was the one with the broad gestures and the larger-than-life personality, she seemed able to control him with a look or a word. Already Gilly had heard him say, "Yes, dear," like a man who'd had plenty of practice.

As for Carl Marks, Gilly couldn't imagine why someone who seemed so unsocial would choose to take a group tour of Europe. His slight German accent made her suspect he'd lived there as a child. So why go there with a bunch of first-timers? She never found out since he contributed little to the conversation. After a while he pulled out a pipe and vanished in search of some place to smoke and that was the last they saw of him. Well, maybe he was just shy.

If Carl was difficult to read, Ed was an open book. He'd come on the trip because he was looking for something different than taking yet another cruise or traveling with a large group. He'd seen the Budget Adventures ad in a travel magazine and had liked the idea of being with a more intimate group. He fully expected to make lifelong friends. This was said with a smile for Inge. Gilly figured he'd be content to enjoy a little flirtation with any willing female and collect a store of pictures and anecdotes to share with his pals when he got home. He'd regarded Inge with awe when she said she was an artist, and Gilly would have been very much surprised if Inge didn't take advantage of his admiration.

Inge. Now there was an interesting traveling companion. Looking at the huge fake gold hoops that hung from her ears, the large stones on her fingers and the bright pink fingernails, it was easy to see the woman definitely had a flare for the dramatic. She may have been an artist, but her passion was men. Inge was sitting between Carl and Ed, and Gilly suspected that she would be sitting next to one or the other of them, or the still unknown Royce Clark, for every leg of their journey.

Then there was David. Gilly wondered if he'd wear well. He was certainly friendly enough, friendly to the point of being nosy. She vowed not to tell him anything she wouldn't want the rest of the group to know in an hour. Of course, David didn't seem to mind everyone knowing everything about him. His life was an open book. He was twenty-one, and a psychology major in his senior year at the University of Washington. Like Inge, he was coming on this trip, so he could check out his German roots. Somehow, David Schwartz didn't seem like the type who was into anything as serious as delving into the past. It seemed odd that he wasn't backpacking his way around Europe, staying in youth hostels, and Gilly said as much.

"My parents are paying," he said with a shrug, "so I figured what the hell."

They were probably paying his tuition, too.

As for their fearless leader, who knew? Gilly had asked him where he taught school and he'd simply answered, "In Seattle." How long? He'd told her ten years. She'd asked if he enjoyed teaching and he'd merely smiled and said it was okay. Yep, a real talker that Rob Warsaw. Well, she'd always been intrigued by the strong, silent type. And, unlike Carl, Rob did know how to smile.

Once Ida and Ivan returned, they all made their way to their gate where they found a mob waiting there – travelers anxious to be gone, adults texting, moms jigging fussing babies, children darting through the crowd. And Carl, who was seated in a chair, engrossed in something on his iPad. The first call for boarding came, and the people with children disappeared. Next, first-class ticket holders shuffled in the direction of the door leading to the jet bridge. Finally, the peons were called.

This is it, Gilly told herself. *Romance, adventure. Right. On the in-flight movie. Get it while you can.*

No. She wasn't going to think like that. She was going to have a great time, darn it all, or die trying. At the very least she'd pick up some great souvenirs.

And off they went, on a perfectly normal flight. No dead bodies in the airplane bathroom, no villainous types skulking down the airplane aisles, trying to catch the attention of any of her travelling companions.

But then they landed, and some funny things started happening. Starting in London...

TWO

The Budget Adventurers arrived safely in London, and in spite of their cab driver's attempt to kill them in a traffic accident, got to their hotel with their bodies and luggage intact. Looking at that elegantly decaying structure, Gilly thought she knew why this trip had been such a bargain. *I'm not the only one*, she thought, seeing the look of distaste on Lisa's face. Well, what were they expecting, the Ritz? This was Budget Adventures, after all.

Gilly and her roomie Inge looked around their home away from home for the next three days. The carpet was a faded brown, and ugly, dark orange and gold bedspreads draped two slightly sagging beds. The cheap prints of scenes from Regency England hanging on the walls and the fake wood night stands and dresser reminded Gilly of something she'd seen in a thrift store window once. The bathroom floor was covered with crumbling linoleum.

Gilly felt her spirits sinking. She tried a bed. "At least the beds are nice and soft," she said, lying back.

"Soft beds! I can't sleep on a soft bed," complained Inge and flopped onto hers.

Gilly could. And did. A knock at the door jolted her out of Zac Effron's arms and she sat up and looked around, momentarily disoriented. Seeing Inge snoring on the bed next to hers brought her back to the present. Good heavens! How long had they been asleep? The knock came again and Gilly stumbled to the door.

There stood David, looking as fresh as soap. "Aren't you guys going to the pub with us?"

"Oh, my gosh! We were supposed to meet at six-thirty, weren't we?" Gilly pushed her hair out of her eyes. "What time is it now?"

"Six-forty."

She moaned. "I can't believe we've been sleeping all this time."

"Jet lag," David said knowledgably.

"How come you don't have it?"

"I'm too young."

"Brat," Gilly muttered, making him snicker, then turned her attention to her roommate. "Inge," she called. The sleeping beauty continued to snore. Gilly went to her and shook her gently. "Inge. Inge!"

"Wha..."

"Are you going to the pub?"

"Pub?" The words worked like magic and Inge's eyes flew open. "Oh, of course," she said and stretched lazily. She sat up, and, on catching sight of David, switched to a more graceful pose and gave him a smile. "Just let me wake up," she said, stretching again and throwing out her chest.

Gilly turned to David. "Will you ask the others to give us five more minutes? I just need to brush my teeth and do something with my hair."

"Okay," he said and disappeared.

"Such a handsome boy," Inge murmured.

And young enough to be your son, Gilly thought, disgusted. She grabbed a brush from her purse and ran it through her tangled curls, then gathered them into Scrunchy. A quick session with her toothbrush and she was ready.

Speed was not Inge's strong point though. Gilly came back from the bathroom to find her roommate still surveying the contents of her suitcase. "Maybe I should go down, so they'll know we're coming," she suggested.

"Oh, no. Wait for me. I'll just be a minute," said Inge.

Twenty minutes later they met a clearly hostile group waiting in the lobby. "What took you girls so long?" Clint demanded. "We're all starving."

Even though Gilly didn't like being blamed for something that wasn't her fault, she felt an illogical need to protect her roommate. "I'm sorry," she said as they trooped out of the hotel. "We laid down and that was it. I don't know how I could have slept so long."

"Not because the beds are comfortable," said Clint.

David had been listening to them. "Welcome to Cheap Tours, Incorporated," he said lightly. "We travel cheap and the rooms are cheap."

"Actually, these rooms weren't cheap," Rob said defensively. "Hotels are expensive in London, and this is actually more expensive than any of the other ones where we'll be staying."

"It may be more expensive but it's still cheap," replied David.

If these were the most expensive, what would the rooms at the other hotels look like? Gilly wondered.

As if reading her thoughts, Rob said, "I think you'll all enjoy the other hotels where we'll be staying."

"You've stayed in those?" Gilly ventured.

"Yes. And in this one, too, in fact. It's not the best," he admitted. "But I couldn't have done better than this without having to raise the tour price."

"Well, Mr. Thompson and I like our room just fine," put in Ida. "Don't we, dear?"

"Oh, yes," agreed her husband.

"They do have atmosphere," Gilly said.

"Yeah, an atmosphere of mold," added David.

Rob's eyes narrowed and Gilly, ever the peacemaker, changed the subject.

The group's first night in London was an early one. Rob brought them straight back to the hotel after they'd eaten and sent them to bed with the promise that their next day would be packed with memorable treats.

And it was. They enjoyed everything from seeing the changing of the guards at Buckingham Palace to touring the Tower of London. But only one incident stood out in Gilly's memory.

After having afternoon tea at Harrods with the Thompsons, she and David returned to the hotel and found they had some time to spare before dinner.

"Want to come to my room and split that can of Coke I got at the store?" he offered.

Gilly didn't feel like going out again. David was harmless enough, so why not?

At the sight of the battered suitcase sitting on the bed across from his she asked, "Who are you rooming with?"

David made a face. "Carl," he intoned in a Boris Karloff voice.

Gilly plopped onto David's bed. She knew she shouldn't be gossiping with him, but curiosity got the better of her. "What's he like to room with?" Carl didn't strike her as the type of man who'd be open to sharing a room with a stranger. Maybe, like her, saving money had held a stronger appeal than enjoying privacy.

"He hardly talks at all, and I can't get him to tell me anything about himself." David handed her a glass. "I think he's a Neo Nazi."

"Don't be ridiculous," scoffed Gilly.

"Why else would he have a Hitler fixation?" he argued. He moved over to the desk where Carl's overnight bag sat. "Look at this," he said, digging in with both hands. In spite of her better judgement, Gilly followed him and peered over his shoulder at the book he held.

She read the title in disappointment. "You haven't heard of this book?" she demanded, unimpressed. "Do you know how many people have read *The Rise and Fall of the Third Reich* since it was written?"

"I bet he's got *Mein Kompf*, too," said David. "And who knows what he's got on his iPad."

"I'm surprised you haven't broken into that," said Gilly.

"He took it with him. Anyway, that's not all."

The sound of the doorknob rattling made David drop the book in the bag like a hot potato. Gilly jumped back a step and tried for a look of innocence.

Carl stood in the doorway, his eyes narrowed, his mouth a thin line. "What are you doing?" he demanded.

Gilly felt a guilty warmth stealing across her cheeks.

She looked at David. His cheeks were pink, too, but he brazened it out. "Sorry, Carl. I was just replacing your bag. Gilly and I were wrestling and accidentally knocked it off the desk."

Fast thinking. Gilly wasn't sure she wanted to be cast in the role of dirty old lady horsing around with the kid, but Carl's expression assured her it was preferable to that of snoop. She excused herself and beat a hasty retreat to her room.

That evening Rob took them to visit the scenes of the Jack the Ripper murders. By the time they came back from skulking around the dark alleys of Whitechapel, Gilly noticed that Carl had recovered his sweet disposition, such as it was.

"It looks like Carl's forgiven us," she said to David.

"Only because I moved in with Rob. Carl didn't want to be roomies anymore."

"I can't say that I blame him."

"Him? What about me? Stuck with that weird old guy. I told Dad I didn't want to share a room, but did he listen? He's so damned cheap."

"He is paying for your trip," pointed out Gilly.

David rolled his eyes. "He thought it would be enlightening. At least it gets me out of the office and away from him for a couple of weeks. Summer torture, working for your father," he added with a shudder. "Still, it would have served him right if Carl smothered me with a pillow in the middle of the night. That guy gives me the creeps."

"Obviously, he's not too wild about you either," Gilly said. "You are a terrible snoop. And you ought to write fiction."

David looked insulted and she laughed. But she couldn't help wondering later that night as she got ready for bed if Carl could possibly have something to hide. After all, he hadn't actually caught them looking at his things, only looking guilty. What had David been about to show her before Carl had discovered them?

She didn't get a chance to ask him. The next day was full of activity and she forgot. That night, with the exception of Ivan and Ida, who opted for going to bed early, and Carl, who had disappeared, the Budget Adventurers went to Soho for a glimpse of London's night life. Loud music and drinks. Some things were the same no matter where you went.

Still, it had been fun. Rob Warsaw was a surprisingly good dancer. And that slow dance he'd danced with her had made her feel sixteen again. Maybe this trip wouldn't be such a waste of money, after all. Ivan and Ida should have come, she concluded. If they kept ducking out on things they were going to miss all the excitement.

The next morning Ivan and Ida and Carl were the only ones not suffering from a hangover. Maybe they hadn't missed so much after all, Gilly decided as she popped an aspirin.

The group left London for Dover, then took ship for Amsterdam, where Gilly watched in terror as their rented van sped down that city's narrow streets, madmen roaring at them from all directions. Hard to believe anything could be worse than London, but this was.

And they seemed to be lost, driving in circles, crossing back and forth over canals. She was beginning to feel like the Flying Dutchman. (Or was that Dutchwoman? Dutch person?)

But Rob knew what he was doing, after all. "Here we are," he announced, pulling up to a curb, "The Hotel Trianon."

The group let out a collective sigh of relief. This hotel appeared new, and fairly expensive.

"Alright!" exclaimed Clint. "Now we're going in style."

He was right. The inside of the hotel looked as nice as the outside. Its furniture was Hilton quality and its lobby lush with potted vegetation. Behind double doors to their right Gilly could see a dining room, elegant and inviting with its linen tablecloths, fine crystal, and vases of fresh flowers. The far side of the room held a bar, complete with cute bartender.

After dinner Rob left for Schipol International airport to pick up the last member of their group, the mysterious Royce Clark, leaving them to fill their free time however they liked.

Ida turned up her nose in disgust when Clint suggested the group use their free time to go check out Amsterdam's infamous red-light district. "We'll pass, thank you," she said.

"What about you, Gilly?" asked David. "You want to come with us?"

"And get my purse stolen? No, thanks."

"Oh, come on, Schatzi," Inge urged. "It'll be fun."

"You guys go on without me," Gilly said, smiling across the room at the bartender.

Inge followed her gaze. "I see," she said slowly. "Yes, I think you should stay here."

The others left, and Gilly sat and sipped her coffee. A couple more friendly smiles and the bartender called across the empty room, "Would you like something to drink?"

An hour later Gilly and Hans, the bartender, had been joined by a man who was a professional race car driver (Wow!), and was bound for Monte Carlo. His name was Jan Van Yeck, and he turned out to be very thirsty.

And, after a few drinks, very talkative. He talked about his racing career, the cities he'd seen, and the people he'd met. "Rich, very rich," he said, shaking his head as if he pitied them. "They waste their money on stupid things.... old pictures, books..." He waved his hand back and forth. "Not me. I like to spend money on beautiful women." He smiled at Gilly and continued. "Someday soon I'll be a very rich man. My friends in America, they have use for the things my friends and I can get from these rich... how you say it?... pigeons. We'll all be very rich soon."

"What do you mean?" she asked.

But Mr. Van Yeck didn't hear her. He was busy signaling Hans to bring him another drink. He downed it in two gulps and returned his full attention to Gilly. "Let me see you to your room," he offered.

Gilly decided this was where the fun ended. She was looking for romance, not a hook-up. She slid off her stool and patted his arm kindly. "That's okay," she said. "I remember where it is. I can find it by myself."

"I insist." He threw down some money, then slipped off his stool, draping a heavy arm over her shoulder.

"No, I'm fine. Really," she said, trying to remove.

His arm proved to be unremovable. "It's no trouble," he slurred, weaving across the room, and taking her with him. His weight pushed her off balance, propelling them both out of the dining room at an accelerated speed. They plummeted across the hall and crashed into a tall, dark-haired man in his middle thirties. The man was able to catch his balance and stay upright. Gilly and her insistent escort weren't so fortunate. They landed in a heap on the floor at the stranger's feet.

Fighting the dead weight on top of her, Gilly struggled to her elbows to see Rob leaning over her. "Gilly," he said, "are you alright?"

She pushed her hair out of her eyes. "I'm fine," she said between gritted teeth. "I was just telling this gentleman that I could find my room by myself."

The Dutchman smiled up at Rob. "Well, hello," he slurred. "I was just going to see this charming lady to her room and then..."

"Yes," interrupted Rob, peeling Gilly's admirer off her. "That was very good of you. Why don't I see you to your room?"

The man with him reached down and helped Gilly to her feet. She gaped at the dark, six-foot specimen of a manhood standing in front of her. He wore jeans and sneakers and a black t-shirt. This had to be.... She felt her face turning red as Rob introduced her, trying to make himself heard over the drunken Dutchman.

Brown eyes looked down on her in amusement. "Hi," drawled Royce Clark. "Nice to meetcha."

"Nice to meet you, too," said Gilly, straining her five feet four inches to look the new arrival in the face.

Rob moved off down the hall with his new friend, completely forgotten. Gilly stood still, her hormones racing in all directions.

"I was gonna stow my stuff then take a look around. Can I talk you into putting off turnin' in and joinin' me in a walk?" Royce asked. The way he said joinin' and turnin' made the invitation sound so charming who could resist?

Gilly could, indeed, be persuaded, and promised to meet him in the lobby in ten minutes, as soon as she'd grabbed a sweater. It was all she could do not to clap her hands, do a little victory jig. Six feet of romance had just asked her to take a stroll around the city.

Royce Clark was gorgeous. Even the way he talked was gorgeous. Oh, yes. This trip had been a good idea after all. She'd booked it as a sort of reward for surviving all the aggravation her ex had given her both before and after their divorce. He had finally found a new woman and she'd decided she needed to find a better post-divorce life. This sure qualified as better.

Once in her room, she made a beeline for the bathroom mirror to examine her face. It was worse than she'd feared. There wasn't a speck of makeup left on it. She shook her head. Green eyes were wasted sitting above that cutsy, freckled nose. Until she got rich and got over her strong dislike of pain, she couldn't do much about the shape of her nose, but she could fix the freckles. She grabbed for her foundation and got to work. Then she added some mascara and lip gloss and called it good.

Ten minutes later she and the newcomer were chatting amiably, strolling down Museumstraat past Amsterdam's famous art museums. "Is this your first trip to Europe?" she asked.

"Not if you count a stint in the army as a trip," Royce drawled. "I was stationed in Germany, but really didn't see much. Too broke. Always wanted to come back and see more. This trip is a present."

Gilly's eyes went wide. "A present?"

"Yep. From me to me." He grinned. "I'm a songwriter and I just got the royalties from my first cut."

"A songwriter!" Gilly was properly impressed.

"Yep. The reason I didn't do London was 'cause I wound up having to speak at a songwriting conference," he bragged.

"What kind of music do you write?" Judging from his drawl, she could probably guess.

"Do you listen to country music?"

"All the time," she lied.

"Ever hear this?" Royce broke into song. "Do you feel good now that I feel bad? Are you happy, girl, now that I'm so sad?..."

Gilly had never heard the song. She vowed to start listening to the country station as soon as she got home. "You wrote that?" she said, trying to sound impressed.

He nodded. "Of course, I still ain't givin' up my day job. Been workin' in construction since I was twenty."

That explained the well-toned, drool-worthy bod.

"Hope that's all about to be behind me soon. Meanwhile, though, I'm celebratin' a little. I promised myself that when I got some extra money and got my ex off my back, I'd do something for me."

"You've got an ex?"

Royce nodded. "And two sons. How about you?"

"I've got a girl."

"You got an ex?"

"Doesn't everybody these days?"

"I suppose so," he said. The ex, Gilly learned, was the reason Royce had wound up a transplanted Southerner, living in the Northwest. "Love takes you funny places," he said.

It sure did, not all of them good.

They stopped on a cobblestone bridge and leaned on the stone railing, looking out on the water. "Really somethin', ain't it?" he said.

Lamps glowed up and down the canal, their reflections dancing in the black waters. For as far as she looked, Gilly could see a series of lamplit bridges arching delicately over the sparkling, dark ribbon. In the daylight the canals looked dirty and ugly, but night draped a cloak of beauty over them.

"I'm glad our canal tour tomorrow is going to be a candle-light one," she said.

"Are you one of those hopeless romantics?" he asked with a smile.

"Oh, I wouldn't say hopeless," she replied. "Romantics are never hopeless." She'd finally given up on her husband, but she hadn't completely given up on love.

They stood talking on the bridge until Gilly shivered inside her light sweater.

"Here," said Royce. He took off his jacket and slipped it over her shoulders.

She felt lost in the thing – delicate and girly and valued. It was a nice feeling, and one she hadn't felt in a long time.

"C'mon," he said. "Let's get you back to the hotel."

They walked back in companionable silence. As they entered the lobby Royce asked, "Are the others as nice as you?"

Gilly smiled at him. "They're a very friendly bunch." And boy, was Inge going to want to get friendly with him.

"Any women as pretty as you?"

"I'm afraid so," Gilly said.

He chuckled and followed her into the elevator. "Your husband must've been a fool to let you get away."

Gilly wrinkled her nose in thought. "Nah," she said kindly, then remembered John's new girlfriend, the bimbo. "Well, maybe he was." The elevator doors opened and she stepped out. "Thanks for the tour of the city."

"My pleasure," he replied. "Pleasant dreams."

Gilly smiled as the elevator swallowed him. "I'm sure they will be," she murmured.

And they were. She woke up just as Royce was serving her champagne in bed. She hoped it was a premonition.

"Have you seen the new man?" Inge asked as they squeezed together in front of the bathroom mirror, doing their make-up.

"Yes."

"What's he like?"

Gorgeous. "He's nice. He looks like he's around forty." Probably a good ten years younger than Inge, but cougars didn't care.

"Mmm, I can hardly wait to meet him," Inge said, and smeared more red lipstick on her pumped up lower lip.

The two women were the first two down to breakfast. They helped themselves from platters of sliced cheese, ham, and crusty rolls.... and waited.

Gilly knew Royce had arrived when she saw Inge's face light up like Las Vegas. "So this is our newest traveling companion," she purred as Royce joined them. "How will I ever be able to concentrate on taking in the sights with such a handsome distraction along?"

I do declare, I don't know, Miss Scarlett. "Royce Clark, this is Inge Brueckner," Gilly said, making a reluctant introduction. "She came on this tour to see the Vaterland and find her roots."

"Hi," drawled Royce.

Inge smiled and looked up at him from under her lashes. How did she do that?

The rest of the group dribbled in, Clint complaining about still having jet lag and his wife telling him to man up and deal with it. Rob and David were the next to arrive. Gilly imagined a little of David went a long way. Rob certainly didn't seem that thrilled to be rooming with him, but Ed hadn't stepped forward, so unless the newcomer volunteered to share a room it looked like Rob was stuck.

"So you're a songwriter, huh?" Ed said to Royce after Gilly had made the introductions. "You know Tim McGraw?"

Royce smiled. "No, but I wouldn't mind having him sing one of my songs."

Inge, losing interest in any conversation where she wasn't the center of attention, changed the subject and asked Rob if she was dressed alright for visiting a diamond cutter. She was wearing a short skirt and tight top. Didn't the woman own anything that fit loosely?

All the men at the table used Inge's question as an excuse to glue their eyes to her chest and Gilly found herself suddenly discontented with her simple top and capris.

Breakfast over, the group left the restaurant. Inge latched onto Royce the minute they left and stuck to him like a burr, hanging on his every word (not to mention his arm). But Ed lured her away at the diamond establishment. He seemed almost as knowledgeable as their tour guide, and Gilly watched with glee as Inge took on a speculative expression and drifted over to him.

Clint and Lisa had toyed with the idea of buying a diamond and Ed gave them a large helping of advice. He lectured them on clarity, cut and color at great length. Warming to his subject, he then cautioned them on how easily an expert could dupe them. Inge's eyes widened as he talked, and by the time he'd finished she was practically pawing him.

Clint and Lisa were obviously equally impressed and decided to invest their money in something other than diamonds. Gilly noticed their diamond tour guide was suddenly wearing a very phony smile. No wonder, she thought. Ed probably just cost the poor guy a commission.

The smile completely fell from the man's face when he produced a tray of small, loose diamonds and an overly excited David exclaimed, "Wow! Look at all those!" as he leaned over and grabbed the man's arm. The black velvet tray tipped, and diamonds rolled and bounced off it, scattering along the display counter. The man gasped and everyone sprang into action, helpfully scooping up the scattered gems and handing them to him.

Gilly picked up a couple which had bounced her way. As her fingers closed over the glittery gems she found herself suddenly reluctant to give them back, and for the first time, she understood why Sticky Fingers made such a good name for a crook.

She wondered if any of the others were experiencing a similar temptation and took a quick visual survey to see. David was handing over his share of the loot and apologizing, "I got so excited. I guess I just didn't think. Do they count these before they give them to you?"

Why do you want to know, David? she thought, suddenly cynical.

Ivan and Ida and Lisa and Clint were dutifully handing over their haul, Clint giving David a look of disgust. Carl was sitting with his arms folded across his chest, watching. Ed was slipping his hand in his pants pocket.

THREE

Gilly did a double take. Ed's hand came back out of his pocket as quickly as it had gone in. There was only one thing that hand could have been doing.

What should she do, say, "What's in your pocket, Ed?" Pull Rob aside and tattle? Ed's head swiveled her direction, and she quickly averted her eyes, hoping he wouldn't notice she'd been looking at him.

Good grief! Ed a petty thief. She felt like conspirator as she handed over her diamonds, but excused her cowardice, first by telling herself that Ed was only human, then by convincing herself she'd been imagining things. *I'm getting as bad as David*, she thought. *He wanted to turn Carl into a Neo Nazi and I want to make poor Ed into a thief.* That idea was pretty silly. Ed was not hurting for money. He had no need to filch diamonds. But it sure looked like he had.

Royce picked one off the floor and handed it to their guide. "I think that's all of them," the man said, looking relieved. He quickly brought his dissertation to an end and herded them out into the showroom.

Gilly watched Inge batting her eyes at Ed as the group browsed among the glass cases and ogled the jewelry. Honestly, the woman had no shame. *Just give her what's in your pocket, Ed.*

"Disgusting, ain't it?" said Royce.

"Do you read minds?"

"Only faces, and yours reads like a grade school primer." He nodded in Ed and Inge's direction. "Don'tcha believe in gold diggin'?"

Gilly shrugged. "I guess there's no harm in trying." She had to admit, Inge certainly deserved the proverbial "A" for effort.

But that was all Inge got. She left the diamond cutter's empty fingered and soon after was back pretending to be Siamese twins with Royce.

By the time they'd gotten halfway through the Rijksmuseum Gilly knew the deck was stacked against her. And the deck wasn't the only thing that was stacked. Oh, who wanted big boobs anyway?

She stood frowning at a painting of a dead rabbit and thought of the upcoming canal tour. Candlelight, wine, romance – she'd probably get stuck with Ed. To think she'd paid all that money to see the canals of Amsterdam by candlelight. With Ed, the diamond thief.

Gilly's stomach began to fidget. How could she hold any kind of conversation with him, knowing what he was?

Stop it! she scolded herself. *You don't know for sure that he took any diamonds. You hardly know the man and it's not fair to jump to conclusions.* All the same, she determined not to wind up sitting with him that night when they went on their cruise.

So much for determination. She not only got Ed. She got David, too. They planted themselves on each side of her as the group got on the boat, and the best general in the world would never have been able to outmaneuver them. Gilly smiled weakly and looked out at the dark waters reflecting the lamp-lights from the streets above the canal. Wine, cheese, candle-light. It was all so romantic. She stole a glance at Inge and Royce and hoped Inge would get seasick and throw up on him. The way she was acting, laughing and tossing her hair, cuddling up to him to take a selfie, made Gilly want to throw up.

Their fearless leader would have made a nice consolation prize, Gilly thought wistfully, remembering their slow dance in the Soho club. But he was sitting an aisle away. Obviously not interested. She should have stayed home and redone her kitchen. Or taken Mandy to Disneyland. This was what she got for being selfish.

After the tour, Royce grabbed her arm as they were getting off the boat. "How about coming down to the bar and meeting me for a drink?" he whispered.

She looked at him in amazement. Did he really think she'd go sneaking down to the bar to meet him after he'd ignored her all day? She may have been divorced but she wasn't desperate.

Not desperate, just thirsty. She slipped out while Inge was in the bathroom and made her way downstairs. Royce was already waiting for her at the bar, watching Hans the bartender perform a card trick. "What'll you have?" he asked.

"Plain Coke," she said, and Hans got busy.

Royce smiled at her and took a swig from his drink. "Thanks for coming."

"Why didn't you ask Inge?"

"I've had enough of Brunhilde for one evening. The muscles in my legs are sore from dodging her all night. I spent most of that cruise trying to keep her foot outta my pant leg."

Gilly gave a snort and picked up her glass of Coke.

"How long have you been divorced?" asked Royce.

"About two years."

"Two years, huh. How come a pretty little thing like you ain't found somebody and remarried yet?"

"Been too busy working."

"Are the men where you work blind?"

"I own a house cleaning business. It's not exactly the kind of job where you meet a lot of men."

Royce shook his head. "You look like you oughta be doing something classy like advertising or selling stocks and bonds."

She shrugged. "I was never much for the corporate world." And the corporate world hadn't been much for her either, not with her degree in history. "It's not sexy but it's good money. Anyway, it's not as bad as it sounds. I don't actually clean the houses myself anymore."

"I sure can't picture you cleaning houses. You're too good lookin'."

Talk about good looking, thought Gilly, admiring the tall, firm body sitting next to her.

She suddenly felt anxious. *What are you getting nervous about?* she chided herself. *Isn't this what you wanted? Here it is, romance with a capital 'R'.* But after divorce with a capital 'D'..... Time to go. "Thanks for the drink," she said, rising.

Royce threw some bills on the counter and followed her. "How about a quick walk to those canals you're so wild about. It's still early."

"Well...." Gilly hesitated.

"You're not sleepy yet, are you?"

Before she could reply, she found herself propelled out the hotel doors and onto the streets.

"I sure could get used to this traveling abroad," Gilly said as they ambled along.

"Me, too," he said.

"You'll probably end up in Nashville now that you're a

successful songwriter," she told him. Another reason not to let things get serious with this big 'ol country boy.

What was Nashville like?

"I already spend a lot of time there. Got some friends I stay with. I'll probably be moving there permanently come fall. Ever been to Tennessee?"

She'd never been much of anywhere. She shook her head.

"Bet you'd love it. Hot music, hot summer nights."

Hot sex. "I bet I would," she murmured.

They found the bridge where they'd stopped the night before. Royce caught her hand and led her to the middle of it. They stood in silence, admiring the view. "I think I could get used to being a member of the jet set," she said finally.

"Yeah? Me too." He smiled down at her and put an arm around her. "You're a nice lady. I think I'm gonna enjoy getting' to know you."

Gilly looked up to smile at him and wound up getting kissed. Nothing passionate. Just a nice, soft, getting-to-know-you kiss. She smiled. This was better than the candlelight tour. And definitely better than redoing her kitchen. Royce was right. She probably would like Nashville.

They stayed awhile longer on the bridge, then made their way back to the hotel. They were almost there when they ran into Ed, coming from the other end of the street. He looked slightly embarrassed when Royce called hello and was quick to explain he'd just been out for an evening's stroll. As soon as they got into the lobby he said goodnight and ducked into the bar.

"He almost acted like he wished he hadn't run into us," said Gilly.

Royce shrugged. "He probably did."

The image of spilling diamonds flashed before Gilly's mind. Ed's hand slipping in and out of his pocket. How many of those little gems *had* he scooped up? And where had he just been, selling stolen goods in some cobblestoned alley?

"I wonder where he was," she mused.

"Who knows?" said Royce. "The red light district? Maybe he slipped out for a quickie."

"Seriously?" The thought of Ed visiting the red light district... no, there was a thought she didn't want to entertain.

"It's possible."

Yes, it was, but eew.

"You're makin' that face again," Royce teased.

"The idea is so... off-putting."

"Hey, boys will be boys."

"Boys will be bad," she countered.

"Hey, now, that's not a bad song hook," he said thoughtfully.

"You want to write a song about hookers?"

"Naw, just want to use that sentence. Boys can find all kinds of ways to be bad, you know. Just ask their women."

"That sounds a little cynical."

He shrugged. "Guess I am a little cynical. But I'll probably get over it. With some help," he added, giving her a wink. "Wanna help me?"

"I might," she replied coyly and he chuckled.

Then he gave her nose a playful tap. "See you tomorrow."

Ah, yes, tomorrow was looking good, she decided as she watched him walk down the hall to his room.

Back in her room, Gilly found Inge in bed with a copy of *Cosmopolitan.* "Where were you?" she asked.

"Down at the bar," said Gilly. "I had a nightcap with Hans." It wasn't a lie. Hans had been there, too.

She took out the postcards she'd been carrying with her since London and addressed one to Mandy, then sent her a gushy text. After that she texted Janet. Tour is going great. Have met some very interesting people.

Boy, that was an understatement. Was she imagining it, or was she traveling with an incredibly strange collection of yo-yos? Ed appeared to be a kleptomaniac. Inge was a nymphomaniac. Carl was... what? There must be a word for him, but she didn't know it. David was a snoop. She would be very much surprised if he got through the trip without someone strangling him.

Gilly dismissed all thoughts of her companions (except one), and went back to her text. Having fun. Expect to have even more before the trip's over.

The next day Gilly decided she'd write a sequel to Dickens' *Great Expectations* and call it *Great Disappointments*. It was all she could do to keep from grinding her teeth when she came down to breakfast only to discover that Inge had already dragged Royce, as well as Ed and Carl off on a bus tour of Edam and some of Holland's few remaining windmills.

"Are you feeling better?" asked Lisa.

"What do you mean?"

"Inge said you had a headache and wanted to sleep in."

"That scab," Gilly muttered. "No. I feel fine. It just took me awhile to get into the bathroom this morning." Considering the fact that her roommate had gotten in it before her and locked herself in while she got beautiful. A very sneaky strategy.

Lisa gave Gilly a sympathetic smile. "Why don't you come sightseeing with Clint and me?" she offered.

"Alright," she said, trying to put some enthusiasm into her voice. She turned to David. He may have been a terrible snoop but he was also fun. "Want to come with us?"

He declined the offer, informing everyone he was going to go shopping. His announcement earned him a disgusted look from Clint.

Shopping sounded like fun, but Gilly was anxious to explore the beautiful old city that had its origins in the twelfth century when fishermen living along the banks of the river Amstel first built a bridge across the waterway. And she wanted to see the Anne Frank house.

Lisa and Clint turned out to be good, if exhausting company. After exploring every possible corner of the city, including some souvenir shops at Lisa's insistence, she left them late in the afternoon and limped back to her hotel room so her tired feet could recuperate.

She took a shower and slipped into her bathrobe, a short satin number, then flopped onto her bed with a travel brochure and began to idly scan it. She made it halfway through before she dozed off.

Heavy knocking startled her awake. Was that her door? She sat up, listening. The door of the room next to hers opened and she heard muffled voices coming from David and Rob's room. Maybe Rob had an acquaintance in town.

The voices next door became increasingly louder and Gilly's heart began to thump nervously. This didn't sound like a friendly visit. Was somebody in trouble? What should she do? A loud crash made her jump. Somebody was definitely in trouble!

Not knowing what she could do to help, but determined to try, she ran next door. The door opened as she grabbed for the handle, and the bulky figure of a man filled the doorway.

If there was such a thing as a Dutch gangster, this guy was it. He had curly blonde hair, beady blue eyes, and a pug nose. His thin lips were pulled down in an angry frown that looked permanent.

Gilly's mouth dropped open and she fell back a step. The man pushed past her and stalked off down the hall. She stood for a moment, hyperventilating, then dashed through the door, trampling David in the process.

"Gilly! What are you doing here?" he demanded, rubbing his foot.

"What do you mean what am I doing here? What did that man want?"

David shook his head, obviously puzzled. "He was looking for someone. I guess he got his rooms mixed up."

"I heard a crash. What happened?"

David pointed to the broken lamp laying on the floor. "The guy has a temper. He started yelling when I told him I couldn't understand him. And he managed to knock that lamp over, too. Do you think we'll have to pay for it?"

Gilly shook her head. "I don't know, but if I were you I'd be glad he took a swing at the lamp instead of you."

David shuddered exquisitely, shaking off the experience, then said an airy, "Oh, well." He pointed to Gilly's attire, asked, "Were you asleep?"

"I was resting," she said, not wanting to admit to being so weak as to have to resort to naps.

"Nice resting outfit," he said, waggling his eyebrows and making her roll her eyes. "Want to go down to the bar and have a drink?"

She was too fully awake now to sleep. *May as well do something*, she told herself. Anyway, perhaps the race car driver was still around. She didn't want to be escorted to her room, but she wouldn't object to being flirted with some more.

Hans stood at his usual station when they walked into the dining room, and he welcomed them with a smile. He had learned Gilly's preference and began pouring her Coke.

Her eyes fell on the paper laying folded on the bar. "Van Yeck!" she exclaimed.

"Bless you," said David.

She grabbed the paper and studied the picture. "That's the man I met. Right here in this bar! What does this say, Hans?" she asked, pointing to the headline.

"It says, 'Van Yeck sought for questioning'."

"Questioning!" echoed Gilly. "Questioning for what?"

Hans read further. "He is wanted for questioning about the disappearance of some, er, how you say? Valuable ... rare books from a...." He stopped, trying to think of the word. "It is the same word you use for 'keep out'."

"No trespassing," guessed David.

Hans shook his head. "It's a....private! Private collection."

"Rare books from a private collection," said Gilly thoughtfully. "You mean he's a thief?"

Hans shrugged. "Maybe. They talk to him, anyway, and find out."

Gilly set down the paper. "Gosh. He seemed so nice. Why would he get involved in something criminal?"

Excitement, maybe," Hans said.

"I can't imagine someone who raced cars needing excitement," Gilly observed.

Again, Hans shrugged. "Maybe he needed more."

David agreed. "A person can never have too much excitement."

He talked on, but Gilly stopped listening. She finally excused herself.

Inge and Ed entered the dining room as she was leaving and she directed them toward David, then left, her mind full of thoughts of Jan Van Yeck. Life was full of strange coincidences. Only two nights before she'd been propositioned by a crook. And now ...

Hmm. Van Yeck had been staying in the hotel. Had David's visitor been looking for him?

Gilly refused to let her mind travel any further. *Don't be ridiculous*, she told herself. *Quit trying link a couple of totally unrelated incidents.*

She picked up the travel brochure to read herself to sleep and tried not to think what might happen to poor Jan Van Yeck – or what could have already happened to him.

FOUR

The following morning Gilly learned from Inge that several of her traveling companions, including Royce, had gone out for a night on the town after she'd left the bar. "Why didn't you wake me?" she demanded.

Inge looked penitent. "I tried, Schatz. You put your pillow over your head, so I gave up. Gilly raised a dubious eyebrow, and Inge rushed on. "Anyway, you didn't miss much. Ivan and Ida didn't come. And Rob didn't come with us, either. He'd gone out to look up some old friend, which I don't think was right. He is our tour guide, after all."

"I don't know," said Gilly. "Maybe he figured he doesn't have to babysit us every minute. Anyway, it sounds like you had plenty of male companions," she added sourly.

"The other men were too busy staring at the hookers to be much fun," Inge said, sounding a little sour herself.

Gilly frowned in disgust. "I can't believe you went to the red-light district again."

"It's interesting," Inge insisted. "You know, we actually lost

Ed and David. They ducked into one of those sex shops when nobody was looking and didn't catch up to us for over an hour."

Gilly couldn't help wondering how Inge managed to miss out on that side trip. Probably too busy hanging on Royce, she concluded bitterly.

We'll see who hangs onto who today, she thought. She got dressed in record time and was out of the room before Inge was even finished putting on her makeup.

Gilly considered it a good omen when she found Royce already in the dining room. And alone.

"Hi," he called. "How'd you sleep?"

"Like a log, apparently. Where's everybody else? I thought we were going to get an early start this morning."

"Ivan and Ida already ate. Ida had some post cards she wanted to mail and they're out looking for a post office. Rob ate, too. He came down looking like he'd been on an all-night binge. I don't know where he is. Carl ate and ran, and I ain't seen nothing of Ed. He's probably still getting pretty for Inge."

"She's primping, too. Did you all have fun looking at windmills yesterday?" Gilly asked casually.

Royce made a face. "Where were you when I needed you? They dragged me all over Holland. And whenever Ed's back was turned I had to fight off Brunhilde."

"Poor boy," Gilly said unsympathetically.

"So what happened to you last night? Ed said you were coming with us, but I got down to the lobby and you weren't there. I suppose you went out looking for your buddy from the bar," he teased.

"Did you hear about him?" Gilly asked, hoping if she shared her wild theories with Royce he'd tell her she was imagining things.

At that moment David joined them and claimed center stage.

"You look like death warmed over," Royce told him.

"I've got a headache."

"Here," said Gilly, filling his cup. "Have some coffee."

"I need a nap," he moaned.

She patted his shoulder. "You can take one in the van."

"On your shoulder?" he asked. She frowned and shook her head at him and he gave her a puckish grin in return and changed the subject. "Guess who did some shopping in a head shop."

"You?" she guessed.

"Carl," he said. "I told you that man had something to hide."

"What did he get?"

"I don't know. He wouldn't show me."

"That doesn't mean he had something to hide," said Gilly. "He just hates nosy people. Anyway, you know he smokes a pipe. He probably bought himself a fancy one."

"Yeah, like a hookah."

"Do you even know what goes in a hookah?" Royce teased.

"Well, okay, so maybe he was buying something stronger. And deadly."

Gilly shook her head. "Poor Carl. Now he's not just a Nazi, he's a drug crazed one."

"He's probably going to try and smuggle something back into the country," David continued, warming to his subject. Inspiration hit and he grabbed Gilly's arm. "Wouldn't it be great if we caught him?"

"You have an amazing imagination," she said.

"You ask him what he bought," David challenged. "See if he'll tell you."

"Hey, marijuana's legal here, and it is in a lot of states back home, too," Royce reminded him. "Including Washington."

"Yeah, but I bet he couldn't get it through customs," David

argued. "Anyway, it could have been something else, something stronger."

"Or somethin' for recreational use while we're here," said Royce.

"Which is probably the case," Gilly said.

At that moment Inge strolled into the room, a vision in a body con sun dress that threatened indecent exposure if she bent over. The color of her nails had changed from pink to red to match it. Her lips, too, were red – red enough to say, "Look at us first." Inge should have had her own reality show. *Real Cougars of the Northwest.*

Catty, Gilly scolded herself. *Don't judge Inge for being flamboyant. You, too, could have red lips and nails if you wanted.*

But she didn't want. Not that she didn't like looking good. She simply wasn't into extremes. There would be no reality show stardom in her future.

"Good morning," Inge sang, sliding into a chair next to Royce. She gave him a coy look. "Did you sleep well?"

"Uh huh," he said and smiled weakly.

At that moment Rob made his appearance. He nodded a good morning and said, "I hate to rush everyone, but we should leave in about half an hour if we're going to stay on schedule. I want to get to Aachen in time to show you the cathedral."

Gilly was ready to go in twenty minutes. She beat Inge to the van and found Ivan and Ida had returned. He and Clint were already stowing away suitcases. Carl stood by watching, puffing contentedly on his pipe. *If this is a drug addict,* she thought, *then I'm a lush.*

But David had planted a seed in her mind and her curiosity got the better of her. She smiled at Carl and said, "I love the smell of a pipe."

He nodded agreement but said nothing.

She tried again. "I saw some shops the other day with some very nice-looking pipes in them. Did you pick one up for a souvenir?"

"The best hand-carved pipes are in Germany," he said, "but I did see a nice one in a shop and bought it."

So much for David's latest theory, she thought in disgust. At that moment Ed came trotting out, and she found herself wishing she could as easily dismiss her theories about him.

"Now, all we need are David and Inge," said Clint. "We'll probably be another twenty minutes waiting for them. Well, whaddya know!" he said in surprise. "We might get started on time, after all."

Gilly turned to see Inge and David coming out of the hotel with more luggage between them than the rest of the group put together. Inge's luggage was plentiful but cheap. David's on the other hand, was designer all the way, including his bucket bag satchel. He hadn't mentioned anything about working his way through college so she suspected his parents were bank-rolling that, just like they had this trip. Obviously, they were financially comfortable.

Gilly's family had been a far cry from comfortable. She'd put herself through college working two jobs. Then, silly her, she'd married for love instead of money. She had the same suitcase as David's but she'd gotten it at an outlet store. Oh, well. Who cared where you got your luggage or what you put in it? Travel wasn't about that. It was about the memories you made and the people you met.

And speaking of people she'd met, she decided she'd have time to trot back inside the hotel and get a morning paper. There might be more news about Van Yeck.

She got a paper and returned to see she'd been mistaken.

Feeling like a reject from Noah's ark, she watched Ida's plump rear end disappearing inside the van after everyone else. As David was shutting the door she caught a glimpse of Royce, pinned between Inge and a window, trying to look happy.

"How about riding shotgun with me?" Rob offered.

Gilly put on her brightest smile. "Sure," she said and climbed in the front of the van, careful to keep her eyes averted from Inge, sitting complacently between Royce and Ed. The woman was man hog.

They managed to get out of Amsterdam alive and once on the freeway the group collectively let out its breath.

Gilly remembered her newspaper and unfolded it, searching for news of Van Yeck. She found it on page two. "Rob, you don't happen to speak Dutch, do you?" she asked.

"Some," he said. "It's similar to German."

"Can you make out what this says?" She turned the paper toward him and pointed to the headlines under the Dutchman's picture.

Rob eyeballed the paper, then turned his attention back to the road. "It says, 'Racing celebrity dead in crash.'"

"Dead!" cried Gilly. "But just yesterday the police were looking for him."

"And just yesterday someone else found him," put in Clint, who'd been listening in.

The poor man, thought Gilly. The poor, talkative, tipsy guy. Obviously, he'd talked too much to someone about something. Who had he talked to, she wondered, and who'd killed him?

Oh, for crying out loud. The man had simply had a car accident, nothing more. That was why no one could find him. He'd killed himself and been lying at the bottom of a cliff somewhere.

Except there were no cliffs in the Holland.

But there were plenty of crazy drivers. And lots of canals. Maybe he just got drunk and drove into one.

Gilly frowned. That didn't make sense, either. A professional driver, used to driving at high speeds having a fatal car accident? She felt an unpleasant prickle run up her neck as a new thought occurred.

"David," she said in a wobbly voice.

"What?" he asked excitedly.

"What if... do you think?... That man who came to your room, could he have been looking for Van Yeck? I mean, the police were looking for him so he was probably into something shady, and that guy looked pretty shady." What if that man had killed Van Yeck?

"Nah. No such luck," said David.

"That man was drunk," put in Rob. "He probably left the city the same night you saw him and that was that."

"Who's Van Yeck?" Inge asked.

"Gilly's race car driver," David informed her. "He got killed in a car accident."

"That doesn't make sense," said Gilly. "Someone who drove at high speeds professionally just wouldn't die that way. Even drunk."

"Oh, look! A windmill!" cried Ida. "Get a picture, Mr. Thompson."

Gilly sighed as the others moved on to new conversational territory. Van Yeck was already forgotten. The poor man. He'd been so looking forward to racing at Monte Carlo.

Conversation eventually petered out as, one by one, the group fell asleep or became occupied with their thoughts. Gilly began to hear snores coming from various corners of the van.

Rob, obviously thinking she needed to be entertained, asked her what she had liked best about Amsterdam.

She knew if she was honest she'd say the highlight of her

time in Amsterdam had been her evening strolls with Royce. But honesty, in this case, was probably not the best policy.

She opted for her second favorite experience. "I really enjoyed the visit to the diamond cutters."

"So you're into diamonds?" he asked.

"I never thought I was. But, somehow, seeing all those sparklies on a tray, something came over me." She grinned at him. "I think it was greed. It was all I could do not to slip a handful in my pocket when no one was looking."

Just like Ed? Should she share her suspicions with Rob?

He was nodding. "I know what you mean. They are beautiful."

"What about the people who work there? Do you think they ever sneak away with any free samples?"

"Not the guides. They're nothing more than glorified sales-people. But the people higher up... Who knows?"

Gilly sighed. "Amsterdam seems to be a great place for enterprising criminals, a real city of corruption."

"It's a large, international city, with a mixture of cultures and languages. Maybe they're just more tolerant," Rob suggested.

"I guess," Gilly said doubtfully. He chuckled and she blushed. "I guess I'm too much of a straight arrow," she said. "Always was."

He nodded. "You look like a straight arrow."

Gilly suspected she was being teased. "Well, looks *can* be deceiving," she said. "You look like a straight arrow yourself. Are you?"

He smiled and murmured, "Of course."

Gilly was intrigued. She spent the rest of the drive trying to pump Rob about himself, but his answers were short, and, being a modest man, he always managed to turn the subject back to her. By the time they passed the German border and reached Aachen he knew the entire story of her life, but she knew little more about him than she had when they'd started. He was single. Divorced, dating someone? Who knew? She still didn't know where he taught German. ("Oh, just one of the local schools.") He liked to travel, and conducting summer tours was a good way to scratch that itch.

Gilly gave up. "You know all about me and I still know hardly anything about you. You're a real mystery man."

He shook his head and smiled. "My life would make a boring mystery. Here we are," he called over his shoulder. "Aachen."

They parked on a small side street and everyone spilled out of the van. "Ooh, it feels good to stretch," said Inge, pushing out her arms and expanding her chest.

Royce's eyes opened wide and Gilly felt a sudden urge to kick him. Or Inge. Or herself for being insecure and jealous.

"There's a good restaurant right down this street and around the corner," Rob told them.

Clint rubbed his hands together. "Alright! Schnitzel here I come." He started down the street at a brisk walk.

"I could go for a thick porter house steak," put in Ed, following after him.

He could afford it. In fact, he could afford a whole cow after that little diamond deal he'd probably made. Gilly couldn't imagine why he felt the need to snitch diamonds when he was already well off.

She sighed. She should have said something.

"What's the matter, dear?" Ida asked her. "You seem troubled."

"If you thought someone was a crook but you didn't have any proof, what would you do?" Gilly asked.

Ida's eyes widened. "Do you think one of us is a thief?"

It sounded ludicrous. Gilly blushed, wishing she'd kept her mouth shut. "It was just a hypothetical question."

"Well," said Ida, "in the first place I wouldn't waste time on a hypothetical question, especially on a trip like this. But, if I thought someone was a thief I think I'd wait until I had proof. Otherwise, the person I accused might sue me for slander." She patted Gilly's arm. "You're thinking about that man you met, the race car driver, aren't you? Well, you shouldn't give him another thought. I'm sure he got just what he deserved."

On that helpful advice, Ida closed the subject, leaving Gilly feeling anything but helped.

They trooped into the restaurant and sat down around a large wooden table. *We look like a bunch of ugly Americans*, thought Gilly, looking around at her fellow Budget Adventurers. They were all wearing jeans or shorts and tennis shoes, except for Inge, who looked like a lost aging hooker. Ed had a fancy digital camera hanging from his neck. Clint was wearing a t-shirt with three stupid-looking sheep captioned *What the Flock?* and his laugh could be heard all over the restaurant. She was wearing cheap sunglasses that no self-respecting European would be caught in. David was carrying around his satchel from which he refused to be parted, claiming it had everything he needed in case of emergency: his sandals, brush and hair gel, change of clothes and his English-German dictionary.

Since their leader was one of those unobtrusive types who blended well with his surroundings, she couldn't help wondering if it embarrassed him to be seen with them. Well, she concluded, that problem went with the territory.

A thick waisted, middle aged woman who wore the traditional German dirndl and a friendly smile came to the table, and Rob ordered for them. Fifteen minutes later she returned carrying plates heaped high with Pommes Frites, the German version of French fries, and thin, golden brown Wiener-schnitzels, all to be washed down with stout German beer.

After seeing the sights of Aachen they headed for their hotel. Everyone got settled into their rooms, then drifted down to the dining room for an evening meal of Wurst and Sauerkraut, a meal Gilly enjoyed, not so much for the cooking, but because Royce snuggled in next to her at the wooden table.

"It's too early for bed," Clint said after they'd finished eating.

"Not for us," said Ida. "Mr. Thompson and I need our rest. We'll see you all in the morning."

Ed turned to Inge. "I feel like a walk. Would you like to look around the town?"

She'd been eyeing Gilly and Royce speculatively. Now she did what Gilly had been hoping she would. She gave up the long shot for the sure thing.

She smiled at Ed. "That sounds like a good idea." She slithered out of her chair and linked her arm through his.

Carl also decided he'd like to see the sights and Inge invited him to accompany them.

"Did he ever tell you what he bought in that head shop?" whispered David behind his napkin as Carl trailed Ed and Inge out of the room.

"A pipe," she said. "A plain, old pipe."

"Oh?" asked David, looking like a man with a secret.

Gilly decided not to take the bait. "Why don't you find those cards you brought, Clint, and let's play some hearts."

"Great idea," he said. "We're always ready for a party. Everybody come up to our room."

If someone had told Gilly a year ago that she was going to become a world traveler she'd have laughed in their face. And if someone had told her a month ago that she'd find herself spending a precious evening of her European vacation doing something as mundane as playing cards, she'd have cancelled her trip. But she sat on the floor of Clint and Lisa's room, losing at cards and loving every minute of it.

"You know," she said to Royce later as they walked down the corridor toward her room, "I haven't had fun like that in over two years. The whole rest of the trip could fall apart and I'd still think it was worth every penny."

"I'm kinda glad I came, too," he said, catching her hand.

She smiled. "You really are a nice man."

"Oh, I can be bad, too," he said with a grin.

They reached her door and he bent down and gave her a kiss that jump started her heart. The look that followed it got the rest of her going. "Sweet dreams," he murmured, running a finger along her chin. Then he strolled off down the hall.

Well beyond pleasant, she thought, thankful she hadn't stayed home and redone her kitchen.

She had just started getting ready for bed when she heard a friendly rap on her door. It turned out to be David.

"Hi," he chirped. "I figured you and Royce oughta be done by now."

Gilly made a face at him. "Don't you ever get tired, child?"

"No, grandma," he retorted and made himself at home on her bed. "I found out something new about Carl."

"That's nice," said Gilly, determined not to take the bait.

"Oh, come on. You know you want to know what I found," he persisted.

"How could you find out anything now that he's in a room by himself?" David's snoopy nose was still out of joint over Carl dumping him as a roommate. Carl claimed he'd never opted for sharing a room. She'd have been willing to bet he certainly hadn't opted for sharing a room with someone like David.

"Ha! You'd be surprised," David said.

Gilly sighed. "Alright. You're dying for someone to play spy with you. Go ahead. Share your secret."

"Okay. C'mon."

He jumped up and headed out the door, but she hung back. "What do you mean, c'mon?"

"I'm gonna show you."

"In his room?" Oh, no. They'd been there, done that.

"You'd better come see this," he advised. "It could be important," he added, as if he'd discovered something of national importance.

She sighed and followed him down the hall, determined to keep him from getting into trouble.

"Where did you get his room key?" she demanded as David inserted a key in the lock.

"I didn't. All the keys work in all the locks."

"Seriously?" What kind of security system was that?

"It's an old place. And they probably figured the tourists would never notice." He flung open the door to the room with a flourish, then pulled her into the room.

"David! We shouldn't be in here," she said in horror as he shut the door. "This is tourist breaking and entering."

"Never mind that," he said, scampering across the room to where Carl's overnight bag sat. He opened it and pulled out a small paper tablet. "Look at this," he said. He flipped it open and walked back across the room to Gilly. "Names and addresses. There's somebody in practically every town we're going to be visiting: Oberwesel, Vienna. He even knows someone in Landsberg."

"So what?" Gilly retorted. "He's German. He's bound to have shirt-tail relatives or friends of friends scattered all over the place."

"Yeah, or he could have Neo Nazi contacts all over the place," David argued.

Gilly frowned at him in disgust. "This is nutty and I'm out of here."

Voices in the hallway stopped her from making good on her threat. Inge's laughter drifted in through the door as if taunting them, and they could hear a familiar male voice as well.

David's wide-eyed expression of panic reflected her own. "Carl," he gasped.

FIVE

"Quick," David hissed, scampering away. "Under the bed."

That was the stupidest thing Gilly had ever heard. People only did that in movies.

The voices came closer and she dove for the bed. David followed her under and giggled and she poked him. If they ever got out of this mess she'd throttle the kid.

A door opened and feet walked across the floor. Gilly heard humming, then the snap of a suitcase being unlatched. The bed pressed down on them. The humming stopped. Peering out from under the bedspread, she saw shoes. The shoes seemed to have grown roots. Why was this man sitting still so long? Had he noticed something amiss? Gilly bit her lip and tried to ignore the prickles at the back of her neck and the sweat pooling inside her bra.

Finally the feet came out of the shoes. Pants dropped to the floor and hands appeared two inches from her nose. The hands scooped up the pants and the feet padded away. Gilly heard the scraping sound of a hanger moving in the closet then saw the feet walk past the bed again. The humming resumed and moved off into the bathroom to be accompanied by the sound of running water. The bathroom door shut, muffling the sound, signaling safety.

"Let's go," David whispered and scrambled out from under the bed.

Gilly followed him, scraping her back in her haste. They raced across the floor on tiptoe and out the door, David shutting it quietly after them. As soon as the door was closed he began to laugh.

She grabbed him by the arm and hauled him off down the hall. "Are you nuts? Do you want someone to hear you?"

"Since when is it a crime to laugh in the hall?" he said lightly.

"I've never gotten sucked into such a crazy stunt in my whole life," Gilly snapped. "And all to see someone's pen pal list."

"Is that all you think it is?" he demanded.

"Of course that's all it is. What else could it be?"

David looked disgusted. "You have no imagination," he said, and stomped off down the hall.

The imagination she didn't have kept Gilly awake long after Inge began to saw logs. That crazy David! How could she have been so stupid as to let him drag her into such an adolescent prank? What would they have done if Carl had discovered them under his bed? What could they have said?

What about that list? Gilly chewed her lip. Could Carl possibly enjoy skating on the wrong side of the law or was he merely the kind of social misfit people enjoyed labelling as a villain?

She finally decided she'd been had. Darn David anyway! Seeing Europe for the first time ought to have been enough excitement for anyone, so if he was going to go around manufacturing adventures he could count her out. With that resolution made, she was at last able to roll over and find sleep.

"You know," said Inge the next morning, "Carl is awfully sweet."

"Yeah?" Gilly wondered how sweet he'd have been if he'd caught her and David in his room.

Inge nodded. "He lost his wife a year ago. He's really very lonely, you know. I feel sorry for him. He's so shy. His wife was the one who did all the talking, kept the friends coming over. I think he wants to find a new wife."

"A new wife, huh? Are you interested?" asked Gilly.

"Me? Heavens, no," said Inge. "He's too serious for my taste."

Well, thought Gilly, at least that explained Carl's reticence. Poor man. Alone and adrift in the social whirl. Maybe he'd taken this tour in the hopes of making new friends. He was probably finding it a great strain. She vowed to be especially nice to him the rest of the trip.

The group got an early start and was on the road by eight. And this time Gilly had no complaints about the seating arrangements. She had settled herself beside Carl, determined to find out all about him. Until Royce seated himself on the other side of her with a wink. Who cared about Carl, anyway?

She didn't, but she did feel guilty enough about the night before to give him some of her attention.

His conversation wasn't exactly sparkling. Was he enjoying their trip so far?

"Oh, yes."

Gilly tried again. Where was his family from?

"Canada."

Oh. She'd thought he was German.

He was, but his mother had settled in Vancouver. He gave

Gilly a small smile and then looked out the window. End of conversation.

She gave up. It was much easier talking to Royce, who kept her entertained with stories of his adventures with the country band he played with on weekends.

By lunchtime everyone was ready for a stop. The air conditioning in the van wasn't working well and Gilly's fellow travelers looked as wilted as she felt.

"I'm so hot," Inge complained, fanning her top in and out, her boobs playing peek-a-boo with all the men on board. "I could strip off everything right now," she added, and Ed looked hopeful.

"Do you mind?" Ida snapped at her.

"What?" she responded, and Ida sniffed in disgust.

Gilly felt the same way as Inge though, and was more than ready for a Limonade, a favorite German soft drink.

Their lunch stop was a quick one, and they barely had time to fill up on Bratwurst and Kraut before their leader loaded them into the van and set off for Oberwesel, an old touristy town on the left bank of the Rhine.

"That's the place where the castle is, isn't it?" asked Lisa.

Also one of the towns where Carl supposedly had a mysterious contact.

"Yes, it is," said Rob. "I think you'll all enjoy staying there. It's one of several castles along the Rhine that have been turned into hotels."

Staying in a castle. If that wasn't the ultimate tourist experience Gilly didn't know what was.

Traffic slowed them down considerably, and it was close to four when the Rhine finally came into view. But it was well worth the wait, an almost blue river flanked on either bank by mini-mountain ranges terraced with grape vines, little villages nestled at their base every few miles. High atop one hill sat an impressive stone edifice.

"Here's Oberwesel," Rob finally announced. "And there's our hotel."

"Oohs" and "Aahs" went up from the group as they crossed the railroad tracks into the picturesque town and began winding their way up the steep incline to the castle.

Finally Schloss Schönberg burst into view – an impressive old stone structure with a modern hotel built into it. Still "oohing" and "aahing" the group piled out of their sauna on wheels, stretching and pulling at their damp clothes.

"Leave the luggage," said Rob, heading for the entrance. "They'll send a cart for it."

They followed him up a small path and through a stone archway. Into another world, thought Gilly, looking at the stone battlements and cobblestone courtyard. Who cared if the A.C. was acting up in the van. This was great!

At the reception desk Rob began a rapid-fire conversation in German with the desk clerk. Gilly listened, both fascinated and pleased with how much of the conversation she could understand: Reserviert - reserved; Zimmer - room; wilkommen - welcome.

"Ich habe einen Brief für Sie," said the desk clerk, handing Rob an envelope. He took it and folded it, quickly stuffing it in his pants pocket.

"Good thing there are other single men on this trip," Inge whispered to Gilly. "It looks like this one was already taken. Getting love letters from home."

"Is that all you think about?"

Inge looked at her like she was crazy. "You know anything more interesting to think about?"

Gilly couldn't think of anything right off hand, but she wasn't about to admit that to Inge.

Meanwhile, Rob was trying to get the room keys passed out. "Let's see," he began, consulting a list.

Clint snatched a key out of his hand. "This looks lucky."

"Clint!" reproved his wife, frowning at him.

"Wait a minute. We all have assigned rooms," Rob protested.

"All the rooms are probably the same, anyway, no matter where they are," Clint said, and began striding off down a hallway.

"Good point," said Ed. "Just give me a key." He took another one.

Irritation and frustration mingled on Rob's face. Poor man, thought Gilly. He did like having everything under control. He checked the number on the keys and gave one to Ida.

She looked at it dubiously. "Where is this room? Does it have an eastern exposure?"

"I don't know now," Rob said, exasperated.

"I think you've put us in the wrong room. Mr. Thompson can't have a room with an eastern exposure. Remember? The sun wakes him. We'll have to exchange rooms with someone."

"Just a minute," said Rob. "Let me think."

Inge wasn't about to give him time to think. She, too, snitched a key, and was already halfway down the hall even as Rob protested that she had the wrong room. "We'll be fine," she called back. C'mon Schatzi. Let's go see what our room looks like."

Gilly gave up waiting for Rob to restore order and followed Inge.

Their room was a lovely one; small, but with leaded glass windows and a tiny balcony overlooking the Rhine.

Inge was inspecting the bathroom (and her face in the mirror) when voices in the hallway called Gilly's attention to the fact that their door was standing open. She went to close it and saw Royce walking by, carrying his suitcase.

"I'm tradin' rooms with Clint and Lisa," he said. "They got a single bed and I got a queen."

What a mix-up, thought Gilly, smiling. This was probably making Rob buggy. She started to close the door when something white on the dresser caught her attention. It was a plain white envelope. For tips? She picked it up. No mention of that. Hmm. There was no name on it.

She opened it and read the note inside. Or tried to read it. It was in German and the scrawl was irritatingly impossible for her to decipher. "Wir haben"..... We have. What was this word? It must have something to do with buy. And the word at the beginning of the following sentence was German for "don't" but what was that mumbo jumbo following it?

A knock on the door gave her an excuse to abandon her translating task. She tossed the note on the bed and turned to see Ivan and Ida.

"We came to trade rooms with you girls. Our room has an eastern exposure," explained Ida. "Mr. Thompson just can't sleep with an eastern exposure."

Ivan nodded agreement and smiled apologetically.

Before Gilly could say anything a tentative knock announced the arrival of their fearless leader. "I'm afraid there's been a mistake," he explained. "You ladies should have had David's and my room."

"Clint and Inge got him confused," put in David, who'd strolled in behind him.

"I guess," said Gilly. "Royce and Clint and Lisa were all mixed up, too."

Rob fought off a scowl. "We wound up with one of the nicest rooms and I thought you and Inge should have it," he said to Gilly.

"How sweet!" exclaimed Inge, who had emerged from the bathroom in time to overhear most of the conversation. She picked up her suitcases. "Let's go see our new room, Schatzi."

On impulse, Gilly scooped the paper off the bed and put it in her purse. She'd work on translating it in the van when she got bored.

Leaving the others to deal with Mr. Thompson's sleeping problems, they went up two floors and half a winding staircase and found a room with enough atmosphere for the greediest tourist. The antique furniture made of a dark, heavy wood reeked of history, and the huge canopied bed in the center of the room looked fit for a princess. The enormous bathroom was all white, pristine tile and the bathtub with its gold faucet could easily hold a princess and any number of princes as well.

"Look at the size of this tub!" declared Inge. "Oooh, and bubble bath!"

Gilly stepped out onto their balcony and caught her breath. She had never in her life seen a view like the one that stretched before her. Gentle, terraced mountains, that blue-ribbon river, a quaint town. *This is the life*, she thought.

A pang of guilt stabbed her. What kind of parent was she, off having fun, foisting her child on someone else? Her more sensible half told her not to be ridiculous. She needed this vacation. Surely Mandy didn't feel guilty over leaving her mother when she went away to camp. Well, this was grownup camp, so no need to feel guilty.

She did take a moment to shoot a picture with her phone and send it to Mandy. Having fun. Hope you are, too. And then to Janet, View from my castle. Jealous?

Janet texted back immediately. Wow! All you need is the prince.

May have one, Gilly texted back.

Deets! came the response.

Gorgeous and single. Life is good, Gilly texted.

She looked down at the courtyard. Clint and Lisa were waiting there with Royce. He looked up and saw her and called, "C'mon down. We're hungry."

They didn't have to call this little pig to the trough more than once. She hurried downstairs and outside.

Rob drove his group to the nearby village of Bacharach for their evening meal. The town was small and quaint, complete with crumbling buildings, an old Roman wall and cobblestone streets.

After dinner they decided to explore some of those enticing streets. David attached himself to Gilly and Royce, and as they all wandered around town, kept her laughing with silly sotto voice barbs directed at the other members of their group and any town citizen who looked like good comic material.

"There's a criminal type," he said, indicating a lean, florid faced man with a drooping moustache. "Guten Abend," he called in atrocious German.

The man nodded and muttered, "Abend."

Gilly smiled at the man but received nothing in return. Instead, he turned his head away. "You're right," she said to David. "He does look like a criminal."

Rob led them down a little street. "Anyone like to try German ice cream?" he asked.

"Yum," said Gilly, following him into the ice cream parlor, the others falling in behind.

German ice cream wasn't American ice cream, she concluded, but whatever it lacked in taste and texture was more than made up for in what came with it – real whipped cream and a variety of exotic toppings laced with Schnaps.

She was too occupied with the sensations of her taste buds to take much notice of the other customers, but people were David's business. He'd barely made a dent in his chocolate sundae before he noticed the man with the moustache they'd seen earlier.

He gave Gilly a nudge. "Look! There he is again. Do you think he's following us?"

"How many spy movies do you watch?" she demanded.

"Don't spoil my fun. I'm going to go see if he spreckens English."

Gilly cringed at David's pronunciation. "If he doesn't you're in trouble," she said. "And if he punches you in the nose we're not coming to your rescue," she added as he started across the room.

David stuck his tongue out at her and pranced over to the other side of the ice cream parlor.

The man had been about to get up. Gilly watched as he looked in surprise at David and sat back down. "Geez, he's fearless," she said.

"Naw, just young," said Royce.

Gilly looked wistfully at her empty bowl. She eyed David's. "It's melting." She looked across the room. Rob had gone to the restroom right before David got up. He came out and, seeing David with the stranger, looked miffed. He went over and said something to David, who gave him a belligerent look, stood up and stomped back to the table. Rob stood a moment, talking to the man, then followed David.

"Nuts," muttered Gilly as David returned to claim his sundae.

"You didn't get back any too soon," Royce told him. "She was just about to eat your dessert."

David ignored his comment. "Just because I'm the youngest one on this tour doesn't mean I need babysitting," he seethed and stabbed the melting mound of ice cream with his spoon.

Gilly and Royce exchanged glances but said nothing.

"I don't know about the rest of you," said Clint, "but I'm ready to get back and explore the castle."

"Good idea," said Ed.

"Well, I'm not," said David. "I haven't finished my ice cream."

"Hey, if you'd stayed put and ate instead of trying to pick up the natives you'd be done like the rest of us," Clint retorted.

"Stuff it, Clint!" snapped David. He threw down his napkin and stalked out of the ice cream parlor.

Clint merely shrugged as if David were crazy, and the group trooped back out onto the street, leaving behind crumpled napkins and David's melting sundae.

In spite of the fact that David pouted all the way back to the hotel the atmosphere inside the van was one of camaraderie. "We'll be losing our light soon," Rob said as they walked into the courtyard. "But feel free to explore what you can."

"Maybe we should get rid of our purses," suggested Ida. "They'll just get in the way."

"Yes," agreed Inge. "Here, Schatzi," she said, pushing hers into Gilly's arms. "Will you take mine up? There's no sense in both of us going."

Gilly felt put upon, but obliged. Once in her room, she decided on a quick trip to the bathroom.

She was still in it when she heard Ida warbling, "Hallo."

"I'm in the bathroom," she called.

"I just wanted to see your room," called Ida. "It's lovely. But it has an eastern exposure. It would never do for Mr. Thompson. My, but it would be fun to sleep in a canopied bed."

Gilly came out to find Ida on the balcony, a vision in a her baggy shorts and top. She'd added a nubby yellow sweater to the ensemble.

"You might want to get a sweater or jacket," she suggested. "It's turning cool."

Yep. Everyone's mother. Gilly couldn't help thinking of the famous mom joke: I'm cold, put on a sweater. Ida was probably right though. It would get cool once the sun went down.

"Good idea," she said, and pulled a sweater out of her suitcase.

Halfway down they met David coming up. "I need to brush my teeth," he explained.

"Hurry," Ida told him. "It won't stay light forever."

Inge had her handy dandy selfie stick, and insisted on taking a picture of the group in front of the entrance, then they all spent the next twenty minutes clambering to the top of the castle's wall and wandering down shivery, dead end passages. Finally, as the fading light was about to put an end to their exploring, their leader led them down a winding path to a scenic lookout complete with a small, white stone bench. Another photo op. After that they broke up into groups, Inge and Ed disappearing around a corner.

Gilly and Royce leaned their arms on the stone parapet and looked out over the Rhine Valley. The river had changed from blue to black. A solitary car roared down the highway on the other side of it, a distant shadow facing a beam of light.

Gilly watched its headlights disappear and sighed. "I wish I lived here."

"If you lived here you'd probably take it all for granted," said Royce, putting an arm around her shoulder.

"I'm not going to want to go back to my life the way it is by the time this vacation is over."

He nuzzled her hair. "Maybe your life won't be the same after this vacation."

Oh, yes. This what she'd had in mind when she first saw

that Budget Adventures ad in a Groupon email. "Why don't you do like they do in those old musicals and sing to me?"

"I can think of other things I'd rather do to you than sing. Look at those pretty curls." He ran a hand through her hair, moved it aside and planted a kiss on her neck that made her tingle. "Let's go check out that Gazebo with the great view I saw on the other side of the bridge," he murmured.

Gilly was into views. Among other things. "Good idea," she said.

Holding hands, they strolled out of the courtyard and past the parking lot. *If it wasn't for the cars over there,* Gilly thought idly, *we could be in another century.* Looking at the cars, she realized something wasn't right.

And with a sudden, sick feeling, she knew what it was. She stopped dead in her tracks and turned to Royce. "Our van's gone!"

SIX

Royce stared in disbelief at the empty space where they'd last seen the van. His mouth set in a thin line. "It looks like the gazebo will have to wait," he said.

"Who would steal a van?" Gilly panted as they ran back across the courtyard.

"Beats me. I just hope we get it back by tomorrow."

They retraced their steps to the scenic lookout. It was deserted. They charged into the hotel. "What's Rob's room number?" Royce asked her.

"I don't know," she said.

"How good is your German?"

"We'll find out." She stepped up to the reception desk and stuttered out a request for Rob's room number.

The clerk smiled patronizingly at her and said, "Sechsundzwanzig."

"Danke," Gilly murmured, and beat a hasty retreat.

"That's not bad," Royce said as they headed for the stairs. "I'm impressed."

"Yeah? You're a lot more easily impressed than the hotel

clerk. You said you spent time in Germany. Didn't you learn any Deutsch?"

"Yeah. Zwei Bier, bitte."

Gilly shook her head at him.

"Hey, I tried," he drawled. "But it never sounded right with a southern accent."

They got to room twenty-six and knocked on the door. No answer. Royce knocked again. Still no answer. He looked at Gilly and shrugged. "Guess that solves the mystery of the missing van."

She blushed, feeling incredibly stupid.

"Hey, I jumped to the same conclusion, too," he said consolingly. "Our leader must'a cut out in a hurry."

"He did have a letter waiting for him when we got here," said Gilly.

Royce grinned. "Tour guides and sailors – a girl in every port. Although these days you'd think he'd be getting texts instead of letters."

"I wonder who it was from," she mused.

"Don't hold your breath waitin' on him to tell you. He's nice enough, but the guy's pretty careful about keeping his boundaries in place. We're a job to him, that's it."

It was all Gilly could do the next morning not to ask Rob about his German girlfriend. *None of your business*, she told herself firmly.

Royce entered the breakfast room and slid in at the table next to her. "Morning," he said. "How'd you sleep."

"Fine. How about you?"

"I had pleasant dreams." He lowered his voice. "Remind me to tell you later what I was dreamin' about."

Gilly blushed and smiled, and he grinned and said, "Pass me that plate of cheese, will you Ida?"

After breakfast the group packed their bags and left the

castle. *Cinderella for a day*, Gilly thought wistfully as they walked out of the courtyard.

The only person missing was Carl. "He's going to spend time with some friends here in the valley," said Rob. "He'll catch up with us after our Rhine cruise."

At this David poked Gilly's shoulder and gave her a "that should prove he's up to something" look.

She shook her head reprovingly at him, but then found herself wondering who Carl was really visiting. *Stop it*, she commanded herself. There was no need to start trying to turn the tour into some kind of goofy movie adventure.

Rob loaded them on their cruise boat and promised to pick them up in Bingen, a town further up the river. "I wonder what he'll do for the next two hours," Gilly mused.

"Probably find a place to hole up and get a drink," said Royce. "It's gonna be a scorcher." He squinted down the river as they boarded the boat. "It's a helluva view, but he's probably seen it twenty times before."

"Let's go up above and grab some sun," suggested Lisa.

Royce turned to Gilly. "Okay with you?"

"I'll probably freckle like mad but I'll chance it," she said.

They followed the Madsens up a small stair ladder and settled in at a table on the sun deck.

As the boat pulled away from the dock and began to chug up the river, Gilly leaned back in her chair and prepared to enjoy the next two hours.

Clint stretched out his legs and gave a loud sigh. "This is the life, huh?" he said. "No work, just traveling around the world with a beautiful woman." He smiled at his wife, who smiled back.

"I'm going to hate to go back to work," said Gilly.

"This boy won't be working much longer," Clint announced.

"Gonna rob a bank?" guessed Royce.

Clint grinned. "Better than that. I've made some investments that are gonna pay off big. I'm planning on retiring young and living the good life."

"If you can do it, it's great," Royce said.

"There are always ways," Clint told him. "Most guys just aren't smart enough to see them. They get stuck in the old eight to five and die with their nose to the grindstone."

"Speaking of living it up, why don't you go get us a drink?" Lisa suggested.

"Yes, dear," said her husband, and went in search of beer.

"What's Clint investing in?" Gilly asked her.

Lisa shrugged. "Who knows? Clint's always got something going. He's determined to be a millionaire by the time he's fifty. His family was poor and he's been hustling since he was twelve."

"That's rough," said Gilly. Her family had gone through some lean years, too. Heck, so had she. She could identify.

"He's ready to make a quick buck and retire," Lisa continued. "But don't take him too seriously when he talks. That's really all it is."

The boat chug-chugged on up the river, and Gilly closed her eyes, concentrating on the comforting warmth of the sun on her skin. She didn't realize she'd fallen asleep until her head dropped and jerked her awake. She looked around in groggy embarrassment.

"Have a nice snooze?" Royce asked.

"I guess I got a little too relaxed," she said, sitting up.

"That's okay. Old people always doze off," teased David, who was now installed in a chair next to Lisa.

"Ha, ha," Gilly said, then turned to Royce. "How long was I asleep?"

"Only about twenty minutes."

"It must be the combination of the sun and movement of the boat," she said.

"Wanna go below where it's cooler?" Royce offered.

"I guess I'd better or I'll sleep through the whole cruise."

They left the others soaking up rays and went below. It seemed to Gilly that they'd no sooner gotten settled than their boat began to turn in toward the bank. "Bingen," announced Royce. "Here's where we get off."

Rob stood on the dock waiting for them, along with the much-maligned Carl. Carl had friends here. What had their fearless leader done to entertain himself the last two hours? Maybe he'd been with the same girl he'd seen the night before. *You've been spending too much time with your roommate*, she scolded herself. *Your mind's beginning to run on the same love track as hers.*

They bought some bread and Wurst and pop at a refreshment stand, then kicked around the quay, buying souvenirs.

Gilly finished her purchases before the others and was waiting for Royce when she spied Carl, sitting on a nearby stone bench. She'd go keep him company, find out a little more about him. She wasn't being nosy like David, she assured herself as she cornered Carl and began to pump him. She was merely showing a friendly interest.

"Did you enjoy seeing your friends?" she asked.

He smiled politely. "Yes, I did."

Gilly waited for him to say more. Naturally, he didn't. "Were these some friends you met through business?" she asked.

"No, no," he said, shaking his head, still smiling.

"A lady friend, perhaps?" she persisted, trying to sound coy.

Carl's smile began to fade.

"I know I'm being nosy," Gilly admitted. "I just think it's

fun to know people in other countries, and I was curious as to how you'd met your friends."

"My family still knows many people in Germany," he said. "Excuse me, please. I think I'll buy myself something to drink. Would you care for something?"

Gilly knew when she'd lost. "No, thanks," she said and let Carl make his escape. She watched him go and chewed her lip thoughtfully. Maybe David was right and Carl was a man with something to hide. Why else wouldn't he want to talk about his friends?

"Maybe his family were Nazis," Royce suggested when she asked him. "Carl's a strange bird. I wouldn't be surprised to hear he had a mad Nazi doctor or two perched somewhere in his family tree."

"Now you sound like David," said Gilly. "Do you really think he has something to hide?"

Royce shrugged. "It's possible. Most people do."

"Do you?"

He gave her a sober look and lowered his voice. "I make women tie me up with their panties and feed me ice cream."

Gilly frowned at him. "Are you ever serious?"

"Of course I am. It's a little hard to be serious about this, though. Why are you pickin' on Carl, anyway? Just 'cause he's not a talker?"

"Well, no. Not exactly. There's something about him. I never did tell you about how he pounced on David and me when he caught us looking in his travel bag, did I?"

Royce's eyes widened and a blushing Gilly related her London adventure. He chuckled and put a paw on her shoulder. "You oughta write novels."

"You don't think his behavior was a little strange?"

"I'd snap, too, if I caught somebody going through my things."

"Yeah, you're probably right. I'm just glad he didn't catch us hiding under the bed."

Royce's eyes bugged even wider.

"Never mind," she said. "It's a long story."

He grinned at her. "Looks like Carl ain't the only person here who's a little different." Gilly made a face and he laughed. "It's okay. I like you anyway. And if the urge ever overtakes you, feel free to come hide under my bed. Or, better yet, in it."

It was the best offer she'd had in a long time and she couldn't help smiling. "I bet you say that to all the girls."

"Only the ones who like ice cream," he said with a wink. "Seriously, I ain't been in a hurry to get in bed with anyone since my divorce."

Maybe that was a subtle message to her not to become too attached. "I get that," she said diplomatically.

"But things change. You meet someone nice and it gives you hope. Anyway, I guess you can't hide from love forever."

"Now there's a song title," she teased.

"Yeah, I might have to play around with that. You're good inspiration. You know that?"

"Aw, you're only saying that cause it's true," she joked. Easy to be an inspiration for a country song when your love life had played out like one, cheating man and all. She said as much to Royce.

"Every barn has an ass," he said.

"Hey guys," called Clint. "We're rolling."

That ended the souvenir shopping and the sharing. Rob loaded them into the van and they set off for Heidelberg.

Their stay in that city was without incident, and the next day they went to see the famous Tegelberg Mountain and two of the castles of crazy Ludwig, onetime king of Bavaria.

The Bavarian Alps had been beckoning them from a

distance for some time. Now the mountains loomed above them like silent giants.

"Here's the town of Schwangau," Rob announced.

Gilly took in the neat houses with their small, well cared for lawns, the abundance of flowers blooming in gardens and window boxes, the cozy, cobbled streets, and felt a sudden romantic attachment for the town.

"That's the Tegelberg," he continued, pointing to the east of them. "You'll get a great view of the valley from up there. And it's a real popular spot with hang gliders, so we'll probably see some taking off. It's a little misty right now, but it should clear up by the time we get to the lookout."

A little misty? The mountain was shrouded in fog. And it was already after one. Hopefully, Rob was right and the fog would lift by the time they got to the top. After all, it was nice and sunny down here in the valley. It was only a matter of time until the sun burned off the haze.

Ten minutes later they'd left their van in a large parking lot and walked to a building that housed the cable cars which took non-hikers up the mountain.

Gilly looked at the little metal and glass bubble dangling from the long cable and gulped. "I think I'll wait here for you guys," she said.

"Aw, c'mon," said Royce, putting an arm around her shoulder. "You don't want to miss this."

"Yes, I do," she assured him.

"Come on, Gilly," said David. "Everybody's got to go some time."

But not before they'd finished raising their daughter. "I don't think so."

"Nothing's gonna happen," Royce assured her, and gave her an encouraging squeeze.

She hated to look like a coward or a poor sport. Besides,

people went up and down the mountain in those things all the time. She gulped and allowed him to lead her into the building, all the while praying she wouldn't regret it.

In spite of the fog, the place already held a fair number of tourists waiting to board the cable cars. As Gilly watched the people ahead of them squash themselves into one and go swinging up the mountainside she again had second thoughts. She looked at the restaurant on the other side of the loading area. She could have a nice cup of tea. Or she could go outside, sit in the sun and watch the hang gliders unloading their cars. She took a desperate look behind her, wishing she was going out the exit door.

A few people stood in line in back of them and others milled around the waiting area. A lone figure moving at the edge of the crowd caught her eye – a tall, florid faced man with a tough expression on his face. More German gangster types. David would love this.

She was about to poke him and point out the guy when she realized Mr. Gangster was looking in her direction. He nodded. With whom had he made eye contact? Gilly turned around to see, but no one from her group was looking at him. She turned back and the man had disappeared. *Imagining things again?* teased her saner self.

The line started moving, and her heartrate started climbing. She reminded herself that she was having a once in a lifetime adventure and took a deep breath. Next thing she knew she was swept into the little cable car and hauled up the mountain to hear the unforgettable sound of a man screaming as he fell to his death.

SEVEN

All the way down the mountain, Gilly had been stringing together the seemingly unconnected events: Ed's petty larceny and mysterious disappearance in Amsterdam, the death of Jan Van Yeck, the strange letter she'd found at the castle in Oberwesel. And now this. Surely no one touched the Twilight Zone of other people's lives this often without finding the events somehow connected. But where was the connecting thread?

Suddenly she knew what would show it to her. She slipped her hand into her purse.

The others were busy discussing the accident. Where down there did David think the body of the dead man was lying? Could they see it from the cable car? Had the mysterious man died as he fell or when he hit? How had he managed to fall in the first place?

"It was probably a suicide," said the normally reticent Carl.

"Suicide?" David echoed.

"The man was alone," pointed out Carl.

"But why go all the way to a mountaintop to kill yourself?" Lisa objected.

Carl shrugged and fell back into his customary silence.

"Why not?" countered Clint. "It's as easy a way to do it as any."

Gilly wasn't listening. She was busy scrabbling in her purse, feeling for the note she'd found in her hotel room in Oberwesel. Where was it? She dug deeper.

"Lose something?" asked Royce, and she jumped.

She dredged up a lipstick. "Just this," she said, and smeared some on.

"We'll still have time to take in Neuschwanstein," Rob said. "That's the castle Disney modeled his on."

Gilly barely heard him. She was too busy searching her purse in disbelief. The note had to be there.

At the castle, their guide moved them along at a good pace, leaving them little time to examine the murals and expensive knick-knacks, then left them within wallet's reach of the souvenir shop where they were free to spend as much time (and tourist dollars) as they wanted.

Pretending to look for her wallet, Gilly made one last frantic search of her purse. It was useless. The thing was as gone as their tour guide. She dredged up a phony I'm-having-fun smile for Royce, and they trailed the others out of the castle and down a scenic walk. All the while she kept asking herself how she could have lost that note.

The answer to that question was simple. She hadn't lost it. Someone had taken it.

"Come look at this view," called Lisa.

Ahead of them stretched a narrow bridge spanning a deep ravine. On one side was a view of the castle with the valley behind it, dotted with lush pasture and tiny houses. On the other side of the bridge stood the neighboring mountainside. A waterfall plummeted down a million feet into a tiny, green pool.

Gilly had taken six steps out onto the wooden planks of the bridge when the scream of the man who fell off the Tegelberg echoed through her mind. Suddenly her feet couldn't move, either forward or backwards. She stood frozen while prickles of terror crawled along her skin. What a scrawny little bridge this was. If it gave way how long would it take before she hit bottom; seconds, minutes? She closed her eyes, trying to block out the scene in her mind, then winced as her imagination produced a sick thud.

A fat man walked by her and the bridge shook. She wanted to scream and run but couldn't.

"Come on, Gilly," Royce was saying. "Let's take a selfie with the castle in the background." He moved to the middle of the bridge and held out his arm in invitation for her to come insert herself at his side.

Afraid to move even her head, she could only turn her eyes in his direction.

"What's the matter?" he called.

"I... " She swallowed hard and tried again. "I..."

Comprehension dawned and he moved forward, put an arm around her and dragged her off the bridge. He seated her on a nearby bench and wrapped his arms around her while she shut her eyes and took several deep breaths.

"Thanks," she breathed. "That bridge is just too rickety for me."

"You really do have a fear of heights, don'tcha?"

"A little."

"A little? I'd call that a lot."

"No. It's never been that bad before. It's just..." She stopped.

"What?" he prompted.

"I remembered that man who fell off the mountain, and it was like I could hear him screaming all over again..." Gilly's voice trailed off. She looked at the others on the bridge gaily snapping pictures. She held out her cell phone. "Will you take some pictures for me?"

"Sure. You gonna be alright?" he asked in concerned tones.

She nodded.

He patted her thigh and strode back out onto the bridge.

She watched him go and bit her lip. She should have told him what else was going on in her head. But how could she explain to him why she was suddenly so sure that man's death hadn't been an accident? Or a suicide. And how could she explain the sudden feeling of foreboding that had settled over her, the awful feeling that maybe someone in their group was doing more than simply seeing the sights.

There. She'd finally admitted it. That was the thought that had been creeping around in her mind. Impossible as it seemed, she felt sure one of them was involved in something ugly and that something was rubbing its dark stain on their tour.

This is silly, she told herself sternly. *You're overwrought, overtired, over imaginative.* All the same, she wished she had the ruby slippers Judy Garland had worn in *The Wizard of Oz.* She'd have clicked her heels together and headed home.

But then the next two days went so smoothly Gilly was able to convince herself she'd only lost the mysterious note, after all, and that her wild thoughts had been nothing more than imagination and fear of heights mixed with too much Bratwurst.

Until they reached Austria.

Rob was determined to make Melk in time to tour its Benedictine Abbey. "It's famous for its architecture and its library, which contains eighty-thousand books and two-hundred manuscripts," he said.

"Don't some of their books date as far back as the year eight hundred?" put in Ed.

Rob nodded. "It's impressive."

"When will we get there?" asked David. "Are we lost?"

"No, we're not lost," Rob said, his polite tone of voice sounding forced. "It's about a three-hour drive. We'll make the abbey in time for the last tour at five."

Inge looked at her watch and moaned. "That's another hour and a half."

Clint groaned. "I could sure go for a beer right now. I wish I'd gotten a bottle of something from the landlord at that Gasthaus where we had lunch. Too bad this van doesn't have working air-conditioning."

"It does have air-conditioning," said David. "Here at Cheap Tours, Inc. you get it by rolling down the windows."

Gilly saw Rob's jaw clenching. Obviously, David's little barb had gotten to him. Poor Rob. It wasn't his fault the rented van's air conditioning was doing its death rattle. By the time this tour was over David would either be riding strapped to the top of the van or Rob would have no molars.

"Here," said Ida, pulling some disposable wipes from her huge purse. "Maybe this will help cool you all down."

"Bless you," said Clint. "Is there anything you didn't think to bring on this trip?"

"I don't think so," she replied matter-of-factly.

"What did we do before air conditioning?" Lisa observed.

"Sweated," said David. "Like we're doing now."

"I've got to admit, I sure appreciate all our modern conveniences," said Gilly. "I'm all about microwaves, pizza delivery, and being able to order my latte right from my phone. I don't think I'd have made a very good pioneer," she said to Royce, who'd dragged out his phone and begun noting something on it. "They'd probably have left me behind on the prairie somewhere."

"You do look a little wilted," he said.

She wiped her forehead with one of Ida's face wipes and peered over at the screen. "Are you trying to write a song?"

"Just playin' with ideas," he said. "How do you like this?" He cleared his throat and sang, "Gilly, Gilly, you're a bandit. You stole my heart and I can't stand it. I can't wait to get my hands on you."

Whew. Was it getting hotter in the van?

"Pretty bad," said Clint.

Royce grinned at Gilly. "But pretty true," he whispered, making her even hotter. He smiled and pulled up a game app. "I'll play you a game of trivia."

One by one their companions nodded off while Gilly and Royce amused themselves playing brain teasers. Finally Rob announced, "There's the abbey."

He pointed off to the left at a long, massive structure standing high above the town of Melk. The building was riddled with arched windows and had three delicate spires, one of them atop an onion dome at the end of the abbey.

"It's beautiful!" exclaimed Lisa. "Wake up, guys," she called.

Clint sat up, still half asleep. "Where are we?"

"We're almost to the abbey," said his wife. "Look."

Exclamations and excited chatter filled the van as the passengers once again came to life. They exited the Autobahn and ten minutes later stood at the end of a barren, seemingly endless courtyard.

Gilly saw scaffolding on part of the building and a gray pile of stones off to her left. The sun beat down on them mercilessly. She rubbed her aching forehead. The structure looked so beautiful from a distance, she thought. But what she saw now looked anti-climactic.

"We made it with time to spare," Rob announced in

pleased tones, and started for the entrance. The others straggled along behind him, Gilly bringing up the rear.

Royce saw her dragging footsteps, came and took her hand and pulled her gently along. "C'mon Pioneer Woman. You can do it."

The air inside the abbey felt cool and refreshing, and she noticed her companions perking up. But the heat had drained her. She felt tired and unenthusiastic.

Rob purchased their tickets and they milled around, waiting for the last tour of the day. "It's in German, but if you'll all stay by me I'll translate for you," he said.

Goody, Gilly thought irritably.

They attached themselves to a group of about thirty Germans and entered the first room of the tour. Gilly tried to feign interest in the various articles on display – the small-scale model of the abbey, the map marked with the various locations of the Benedictines around the world, the historical artifacts in glass cases. She wandered from one display case to another, wishing for a chair. The hot, hairy bodies milling around her smelled sweaty and that reminded her that she was hot and made her wish for a cold drink.

The tour guide finally moved them on and they followed him through the various rooms, then out to the terrace to take in the view and fry once more in the scorching sun.

If Gilly hadn't been so hot and tired, she told herself, she'd have appreciated this more. She drifted away from Royce and squinted up at the building, glowing orange in the late afternoon sun, then had to turn away. It hurt her eyes.

The terrace lay along the tip of a rock spur. Far below it flowed the Blue Danube. At least it must have been blue once, she reasoned, looking at the panorama. The blue had definitely taken on a brownish tinge.

She sighed and looked around. She saw Carl, standing

aloof from the other tourists, admiring the architecture of the abbey. Ivan was taking pictures, Ida hovering nearby.

Gilly let her eyes travel the line of sweaty backs leaning along the parapet. Inge and Ed were taking selfies and Gilly watched irritably as Inge roped Royce into joining them. David stood nearby and was digging something out of his satchel – the Brötchen he'd taken from the Gasthaus earlier that day. Oh, surely he wouldn't do anything so tacky...

He did. She watched while he dumped the satchel at his feet, leaned on the railing and casually munched on the roll. He ate half and Gilly cringed as he tossed the rest over the wall. Rob would kill him if he caught him acting like an ugly American. Fortunately for David, Rob was about five people down, visiting with Lisa while Clint snapped pictures of the view.

The tour guide beckoned to the group, and like good little lambs they trotted off after him back inside. Gilly watched David stroll off, talking animatedly to Royce, forgetting his bucket bag.

Ida, the eternal mom, picked it up and followed them.

Gilly returned to the stone stairs they'd just come up. *This is it*, she decided, sitting down. This was as far as her weary body went. If they wanted her to go any farther Royce would have to come back and carry her. She leaned her head against the building and sighed.

"I wish this was a Hyatt and that terrace was a swimming pool," she murmured, closing her eyes.

She sat for another few minutes, her body unwilling to move. "Get up," she finally told herself. It was stupid to sit out here baking in the sun. Obviously, nobody was coming back to fetch her. The tour was going on without her, and if she didn't catch up she'd probably get lost. She'd feel pretty stupid running around the abbey like the lone tourist. With a sigh, she got up and crossed the veranda.

She went through the door she'd seen the others enter and found herself alone in a huge room, its walls lined with books from the floor to its amazingly high ceiling. Gilly looked around her open-mouthed. She walked over to a glass case in the center of the room and stared at the thick book displayed in it. Its description was in German but she was sure it said something about a Gutenberg Bible. No wonder they had the book locked up. It had to be priceless.

She walked slowly across the room and the sound of her sandals echoed in her ears. She opened the door to the next room, stepped in and caught a fleeting glimpse of someone's retreating back and what looked like David's bucket bag.

"David," she called, but all she heard was the sound of running feet.

It must not have been him. Well, at least the others aren't far ahead of her.

She closed the door behind her and looked around. This room wasn't as huge as the previous one, but its walls were also lined with books. How old did Rob say these books were? Some of them had to be very valuable. That was probably why they had them held in with ... chicken wire? Seriously?

Gilly looked around for some kind of surveillance cameras like the ones she'd seen in Westminster Abbey, but couldn't see any. Well, the wire was probably all they really needed. After all, what were the chances that anyone would steal any of these books? Who would be low and sleazy enough to rob a...

She stared at the cut wire and the empty space in the bottom shelf of books to her left, the space the size of two or three books, and gasped.

She raced out of the room and down the steps, her sandals clacking loudly. She stumbled into the church, but there were only a few people there taking pictures, so she rushed through, the beautiful frescoes of the sanctuary a blur, and ran outside into the scorching heat.

At this end of the abbey there were lawns and gardens, but Gilly ran down the gravel walk, too preoccupied to admire them.

She found the group further up the walk, clustered around an ice cream cart.

Royce greeted her with a smile. "We were about to send out a search party for you."

She barely waited for him to finish talking. "The abbey's been robbed," she panted.

The others stared at her.

"One of the libraries," she said, grabbing Rob by the arm. "Some of the books are missing from one of the libraries."

"How could you tell?" asked David. "There must be a million books in there."

"Eighty thousand," corrected Rob automatically. "It does sound a little far-fetched," he said to Gilly.

"The wire covering them had been cut," she said. "And there's an empty space where you can tell there used to be books."

Ida looked shocked. Rob frowned. Clint was the first to speak. "Oh, no," he moaned. "First a dead body. Now stolen books. We'll be stuck here for hours like we were on the mountain."

"Clint's right," said Carl. "I'm sure Gilly thought she saw something..."

"I *did* see something," she insisted.

"But," continued Carl, ignoring her interruption, "there probably is another perfectly logical explanation for what she saw other than theft."

Gilly felt her face growing hot and knew it wasn't the heat or the rushing around that had produced the unbecoming flush.

Nobody believed her. They all thought she was crazy. She suddenly felt crazy. But no, this time she knew what she saw.

Rob appeared to come to a sudden decision. "Clint's right," he said. "I can't afford to lose time. If anything is missing we know it wasn't any of us who took it, and frankly, I'd rather not get involved this time. Let's get going before we encounter any delays."

But Gilly couldn't let it drop that easily. A crime had been committed and she wasn't going to be as gutless as she'd been in Amsterdam.

"No, wait," she cried. "They could still catch the thief. I was right behind him."

Everyone stared. "How do you know that?" asked David, swinging his bucket bag up onto his shoulder.

"Because I saw..." That bag! Gilly felt the hair at the back of her head rising to some invisible static electricity. Was it her imagination or was David's bag bulging more than it had when they first entered the abbey? She'd caught only a fleeting glimpse of a disappearing figure leaving the room, but she remembered that satchel.

Uninhibited, artless David a thief? Ridiculous! There were thirty people on that tour.

Still, had anyone else been carrying a satchel or backpack?

Why, oh, why were those monks so trusting? They should have been making people check their bags when they came in. But then who'd be so bold as to cut wire and steal books? Who'd be interested?

Someone had been. Nervous sweat suddenly burst from every pore of Gilly's body. Amsterdam all over again. Once more she found herself reluctant to start throwing out accusations. What if David had a partner and had already handed off those books? He had to have been working with someone. This wasn't the type of thing he could do alone. And what if Gilly said something and then that partner decided she needed to have an accident of some sort?

She switched gears in mid-sentence and tripped over her tongue. "I thought I saw someone leaving the room as I came in."

"Did you get a good look at the person?" asked Rob.

Gilly flushed and stared at her feet. She shook her head. "Not really. Just a glimpse. A back," she finished weakly.

"Then let's go," said Clint. "Ivan," he hollered and waved an arm. "C'mon. We're out of here."

Rob started for the van, David falling in step with him. Gilly watched them go, feeling like a moral failure. She'd made the wrong decision again.

Royce bought another ice cream cone and handed it to her. "Maybe this'll make you feel better."

She took it and muttered a mechanical thanks, but she knew the only way she was going to feel better was by looking in David's bag and finding nothing there but brushes, Brötchen and hairspray. And the sooner the better.

EIGHT

Gilly felt relieved to hear it wouldn't take them long to reach their hotel from Melk. She was beyond anxious to conduct her search.

"So this Krems isn't far from here?" Clint asked Rob.

"Not really," Rob said. "And Krems is just outside Vienna so we won't have to spend any time on the road tomorrow. Vienna will be only about a half hour away."

"Vienna," breathed Inge. "My great-grandmother's cousin on my mother's side was from Vienna. She was an opera singer." After this introduction Inge burst into song, treating them to a slightly off-key rendition of "Music of the Night" from *The Phantom of the Opera*. Ida and Ed joined in.

Gilly didn't. Her mind was still absorbed with the puzzle of the theft at the abbey. Had it been discovered yet? Would it be in all the papers by morning? Would they be searching people at the borders?

She hoped they would, but so far the border guards checking passports appeared to be a thing of the past. If they were stopped, however, a tour group would be the perfect cover for a thief.

She had to be wrong. David was too young and inexperienced to have mastered the art of international crime.

Which brought her back to her suspicion that he had a partner. The man in Amsterdam. Had he really been looking for someone or had he come to see David? Was David the missing link she needed to connect all these strange happenings?

She sighed and rubbed her forehead and turned to find Royce watching her. "You alright?" he asked.

She nodded. "Yeah. Just too much fun and excitement, I guess." She gave him a smile, then turned to stare out the window. She watched the flat, green countryside roll by, and the crazy thoughts kept rolling around in her mind, staying with her until they reached their hotel.

"The desk clerk says the manager would like to offer us a drink, compliments of the hotel," Rob informed them all as they gathered in the lobby. "So why don't we get settled in our rooms, then meet in the bar over there in about ten minutes?"

The others agreed and ten minutes later they were assembled around a table in a small, deserted bar. "Where's our fearless leader?" asked Royce.

"In the pot," said David. "I saw him going down the hall."

The bartender, a young man who spoke no English, brought over a tray of shot glasses filled with clear liquid. Gilly grabbed a glass and held onto it as if it were a life preserver.

"Gilly?" Ida was saying.

Gilly gave a start.

"Where were you just now?" Ida asked her.

"I'll bet she's still trying to figure out who stole those books from the abbey," teased Lisa.

Gilly felt David's eyes on her. She flushed and clamped her lips shut.

"Why would anyone want to steal some old books from an abbey, anyway?" Lisa continued.

"For money, of course," said Ed.

"But who'd want them?" Lisa argued. "I mean, I could understand someone stealing something from one of these European castles, but what kind of market is there for an old book?"

"Look at all the people who collect first editions. I guess there's a market for anything if it's old enough," Ed observed. "Right Rob?" he asked as Rob joined them.

Rob helped himself to a glass. "Right what?"

"We were just saying how there's probably a market for old books," Ed told him.

"I suppose so," he agreed.

"Those books must be worth something or they wouldn't have wired them in," said Lisa. "That wire was meant to keep the tourists from grabbing a souvenir."

"Pretty shoddy security if you ask me," said her husband.

Jan Van Yeck's words came back to Gilly in a burst of light: "They waste their money on stupid things. Old pictures, books..."

Books, books, books... The word ricocheted around her brain, causing the color to drain from her face. Jan Van Yeck had been wanted for questioning regarding the disappearance of some rare books from a private collection. Jan Van Yeck was dead. Now the Benedictine Abbey was missing some rare books. That was why Jan Van Yeck had been hanging around the Trianon Hotel! He was a thief, too, into stealing rare books and God only knew what else. Probably waiting to make contact with someone. But he talked too much and now he was dead.

Just like the man on the mountain. Hysteria began rising in Gilly. She downed her drink in one gulp. It was either that or start screaming.

Rob looked out the window at the graying sky and said, "It looks like it's going to rain. If you all want to check out our surroundings we'd better do it soon."

Let them go, thought Gilly. *I'm going to find a way to get into David's room and search his things.*

As everyone filed out, Ida patted her arm. "Don't worry about the books. I'm sure they've already caught the thief."

Everyone wanted to think the thief had been caught. That way they wouldn't have to feel guilty about leaving the abbey without reporting the theft. Well, everyone was selfish!

Gilly gave Ida a reprimanding look. "You and I both know that's not true."

Ida looked shocked, then insulted. She stalked off, leaving Gilly feeling guilty for being rude to an older person.

Never mind that now, Gilly told herself firmly. *You've got work to do.*

She let them all get out of the bar before announcing she'd forgotten her purse. "You guys go on ahead. I'll catch up."

"I need to get my bag," said David. "I'll go up with you."

Gilly's heart sank. So much for searching his room. Wait a minute! Maybe she could accompany him to his room. She might be able to distract him and sneak a peek in his bag.

She put on her brightest smile and said playfully, "Just don't make any passes at me in the elevator on the way up."

"And have Royce beat the snot out of me? No thanks," replied David.

As the elevator made its slow progress up to the fifth floor, Gilly began to wish they were staying in the traditional two or three story Gasthaus. David was no longer a comfortable person to be around, especially alone in an elevator.

"Did you really see who took those books?" he asked, the picture of innocent curiosity.

Gilly's heart beat a little faster. "Not really. I just got a quick glimpse – only enough to give me a vague impression."

"Well, could you tell if it was a man or a woman?"

"It was a man." Why had she said that? "I think," she added.

"Do you think..." David grabbed her arm excitedly and she yelped. He leaned close to her, grinning evilly. "Maybe..." He paused for effect. "It was Carl."

The little weasel! Trying to put the blame on someone else. "Carl doesn't carry a satchel," said Gilly. Oh, Lord! Why had she said that? *Quick! Say something to distract him!* "It's been a strange vacation so far, huh?" she babbled. "A dead man, stolen books."

Now, why had she said that? David had been the one who'd seen the dead man. He could have easily been the one who pushed him over. Oh, God. She felt sick. David fell silent for a moment and Gilly prayed the elevator would hurry up and get to their floor. She kept an imitation nonchalant gaze on the door.

"You know what?" he said. "All this would make a great movie."

"Yeah?"

"You could call it *The Woman Who Knew Too Much.*"

Gilly's palms began to sweat. *Forget going to David's room. Just get away.*

The elevator opened and she charged through the doors. "I think there's already an old movie with a similar title," she said, pulling her room key out of the pocket of her shorts. "Only it was a man."

David kept pace with her. "Oh, yeah. Some old movie with one of those old actors. I watched that on T.V. once with my grandma. I can't remember. Did the man who knew too much get killed?"

Killed, as in murdered. Gilly dropped her key.

"Here." David picked it up and inserted it in the lock.

"Thanks," she croaked.

He studied her a moment then asked, "What's wrong?"

"Nothing," she said, trying to look carefree and unafraid.

"If you say so," he said doubtfully. "Wait for me, okay?"

Gilly shut her door and leaned against it. She stood there, struggling with wild theories and even wilder plans of action until a knock on the door made her jump and let out a squeak. She took a deep, steadying breath and set her jaw in determination. If David thought he was going to scare her with more movie trivia he could just think again.

She jerked open the door. "The man in that movie did not get..." she began and blushed. "Oh," she breathed. "It's you."

Royce's tall form filled the doorway. He looked like a guardian angel in jeans. "What was that all about?" he asked.

"Never mind," she said. *Only me going crazy.*

"I got to thinking I'd better get my Windbreaker," he said, holding it up.

"Let me grab my purse," she said, and snagged it from her bed where she'd tossed it.

David's head poked around the corner of the door. "It's a good thing I didn't put the moves on you," he said. "Royce would've caught me for sure."

Royce chuckled and led the way down the hall to the elevator.

There was no more talk about the missing books and Gilly began to relax. Even if David knew she was onto him what could he do to her with all these people around? She wished she'd gotten a chance to look in his bag.

The others stood waiting for them in the lobby and Clint was, as usual, starving.

"There's a restaurant just a few streets down," said Rob. "We'll grab some dinner and after that anyone who'd like to explore the town is free to wander around."

"A lot of the stores are already closed," complained Lisa. "Did my husband pay you to make sure there'd be no time for shopping?"

The others chuckled and Rob smiled and shook his head. "No, and I promise you tomorrow you'll have plenty of free time in Vienna. You'll find some really nice shops there. Expensive," he added, "but nice."

They walked into the restaurant to find it already had several customers, locals who stared with frank interest as the foreigners trooped in. They sat down and ordered.

The others made this process as short and to the point as possible, but David smiled at their waitress and began to slaughter the language. "Gut abend. Ick mukta ein Schnitzel, bitte churn," he said, and Gilly could see Rob cringing. After finishing his speech he grinned at his companions, looking like a child who had successfully recited a nursery rhyme.

The waitress fired something back at him in German and he looked puzzled. "What did she say?" he asked Rob.

"She wants to know where you learned to speak German," put in Clint.

David scowled at him. "Ha, ha."

"She's asking what kind of dressing you want on your salad," Rob said.

"Oh." David turned to the waitress. "Blue Kase." She smiled indulgently at him and he grinned back up at her. "Ask her what time she gets off work," he instructed Rob.

"Oh ho," laughed Clint. "Gonna get her to help you with your German?"

"Maybe," replied David. He turned to Rob, who was talking to the giggling waitress. "Well, what did she say?" he asked.

"She said her boyfriend is picking her up at ten."

David shrugged. "Oh, well."

"Maybe you'll do better in Vienna," Lisa said to him.

After dinner Rob claimed he needed to run an errand and left the group to enjoy their free time, pointing them to an area reserved for pedestrians. A variety of shops lined each side of the wide street, and the travelers wandered along it, looking into windows and comparing prices of the things they saw to merchandize in the states.

David was with Ed and Inge, a happy circumstance that allowed Gilly to stroll hand in hand with Royce and enjoy a peaceful moment. They finally decided to turn back to the hotel and were two streets away when a bolt of lightning jumped across the sky and the long-awaited cloudburst came. The stroll turned into a mad dash as the two of them ran, laughing, for the hotel. By the time they reached the doorway, they were drenched.

"Look at you," he said, pulling her to him. "You look like an escapee from a wet t-shirt contest. You should'a let me give you my coat."

Gilly blushed and pushed back a soggy strand of hair. "I'll bet my mascara's running."

"That's okay. I wasn't lookin' at your mascara," he drawled and bent down and kissed her.

David ran up the steps past them. "Hey, aren't you guys coming in?" he called.

Royce waved him away.

"Well! I guess I know when I'm not wanted," he said.

Royce lifted his head and grinned at Gilly. "The boy's smart, ain't he? Go find your own Fräulein," he called over his shoulder. He took off his slicker and draped it over her shoulders. "We should'a done this a little earlier, huh?" he said.

"Mmm. But then you wouldn't have seen what I looked like in a wet t-shirt, would you?" teased Gilly, and the warmth returned to her cheeks.

Royce smiled and started another kiss, heating up other places as well.

She was vaguely aware of someone walking by them, and as the door opened, she could faintly hear David's voice wafting out from somewhere in the lobby. This was a ridiculously conspicuous make out spot. But who cared? She was in the doorway of a hotel in Austria, kissing the most gorgeous thing since Blake Shelton. Now this was romance! Maybe even love. And it sure beat worrying about petty thieves and dead men.

She shivered at the unpleasant thought and Royce turned Southern gentleman. "You're cold," he informed her. He took her by the hand and lead her back into the hotel. "You'd probably better get out of those wet clothes."

The elevator ride to the seventh floor was a steamy one, and Gilly suspected if they had had a few more floors to go she could have generated enough body heat to dry her clothes without having to remove them.

They reached her room and she half expected to see David poke his head out from the room he was sharing with Rob, which was next to hers. But he didn't. Reluctant to break the mood, she leaned against the door and smiled at Royce.

He planted a hand on either side of her head and grinned down at her. "You need help getting out of those wet clothes?"

That was a tempting offer, but she didn't want to rush into anything. "I think I can manage on my own."

"Okay. Then how about you slip into something more... dry and come over to my room and play some cards," he suggested.

"Cards?" she repeated skeptically.

"Or something," he said with a smile.

Gilly smiled, too. A little rushing couldn't hurt. "I like cards."

He gave her nose a tweak. "See you in a few minutes."

She nodded and slipped into her room, savoring the good feelings Royce had generated. A sudden draft caught her attention and she frowned. Inge had left the window open. Oh, what the heck. May as well leave it. The rain was letting up and it would be good to let in some fresh air.

Gilly stripped off her wet clothes and hung them in the bathroom, then padded back to her suitcase. She pulled out her bathrobe and slipped into it, belting it loosely around her. Maybe she'd take a quick shower before going over to see Royce.

Outside the window she could see a rainbow forming. She padded over and leaned her elbows on the sill, looked out and smiled at the world.

She could hear the murmur of voices from the room next door. She didn't think Rob had come back already. But who else would David be talking to? There was more than one person in that room.

Words from the other room floated over to her. "You're imagining things. She doesn't know anything."

The smile on her face died and her heart began to pound. She swallowed hard and strained to hear more. Not easy to do considering how loudly hear heart was banging around. She could hear the rush of blood pounding in her ears.

There was that other voice, soft and muffled. He must have turned away from the window, because she couldn't make out anything he was saying. She leaned her head out the window and strained to hear, then pulled back.

She'd heard that last sentence clearly enough. "Don't worry. I can take care of her."

NINE

He was onto her. He knew she knew. Oh, no!

Gilly fled her room, ran down the hall, and without knocking, charged into Royce's room.

Casual in jeans and a t-shirt, he lay stretched out his bed, playing solitaire. A look of delight crossed his face as Gilly rushed into his room, bathrobe flapping, and landed in his arms.

"Well, well," he began. "Hey, what's the matter?"

"He did it," she panted. "He knows I know and now he's ... he's... We've got to do something!"

His arms tightened around her and he kissed the top of her head. "It's alright. Nobody's gonna getcha." He pulled her fallen bathrobe back over an exposed thigh. "Unless it's me. Here," he said, propping his back against the wall and drawing her under his arm. "How about you start from the beginning and explain what this is all about."

Gilly looked at the door, expecting David to come charging after her. It remained shut, so she took a deep breath and said in a low voice, "It was David who stole those books from the abbey at Melk."

"What!"

"Remember I said I saw someone leaving as I was coming into the library? Well, it was only a fleeting glimpse of their back and something that looked like a satchel or backpack. It didn't register until I saw David's bucket bag when we were outside the abbey. And then I kept thinking I had to be wrong. But I knew I wasn't. Deep down inside I knew I wasn't." She sighed a jagged sigh and Royce rubbed her arm encouragingly. "And then he and I had this weird conversation in the elevator and he almost seemed to be threatening me. But even after that I didn't want to believe it."

Royce closed the revealing gap at the neck of her bathrobe. "Nice outfit," he observed.

"I'm serious. He's going to kill me. Just now I heard him say I knew too much and that he was going to take care of me."

"Are you sure it was him?"

"Who else could it be? He's in the room right next to mine."

"So's Rob. They're sharing a room. Right?"

"Rob went to run an errand," Gilly reminded him.

"So maybe he came back and you didn't know it."

She shook her head. "You just don't want to believe David could be a criminal because he's so young."

"Well, yeah," Royce admitted. "Kinda lacking experience."

"He's got enough. You know, he never said anything about having to work his way through school. I assumed his parents were bankrolling him. Now I think he's found a way to bankroll himself. I mean, look at his luggage. It's not cheap. Neither are his clothes."

"If he's so rich what's he doing on this tour? Why can't he afford a room by himself?"

"I don't know," Gilly admitted. "Unless the tour is a cover."

Royce shook his head. "Sorry, I just don't see the kid as a criminal mastermind."

"He's probably not. He had to be talking to somebody in his room so for sure he's working with someone. Or for someone."

"Yeah, Ed," Royce scoffed.

"It's a possibility. Ed retired early; claims he made a killing in the stock market. What if that's a lie. What if he and David are working together?"

"Ed's too busy with Inge to have time for anything else," said Royce.

"Maybe. But David's got plenty of time, and he's doing a good job of throwing people off the scent with that flitty, twitty act of his."

"Okay, let's say the kid is a thief and a killer. How's he gonna croak you with all of us around?"

"I have no idea, but you know the old saying. Where there's a will there's a way. I think David's got the will. Now he'll be looking for a way. And I won't be his first victim, either."

"Whaddya mean?"

"That man at the Tegelberg. Remember? Who saw him go off?"

Royce was looking dubious.

"There's a connection," Gilly insisted.

"Look, let's not jump to conclusions," he said. "I mean, we still don't know for sure that any books were stolen."

"*I* know they were." Royce still looked unconvinced. "This sounds crazy," she admitted, "but I'm not imagining things. I know what I saw, and I know what I heard just now."

"Okay," he said, and gave her a hug. "Don't worry. I'll protect you."

A sudden knock at the door made them both jump, and she looked up at him with wild eyes.

"Take off your robe," he hissed and slid off the bed. Her eyes widened further and he waved a hand at her and pulled off his t-shirt, then headed for the door. Gilly slipped out of her robe and crawled under the blankets. Royce gave a quick backwards glance and nodded encouragingly at her, then opened the door halfway.

"Hi," said David. "I just scored some Kuchen from the owner's wife. Wanna play cards?" He looked beyond Royce and saw a blushing Gilly with the sheet pulled up to her neck. "Oh, sorry," he said, a sly smile creeping over his face. "Maybe later."

"Yeah," said Royce, "Later," and shut the door.

Gilly looked questioningly at him. "What do you think he was up to?" she whispered.

"Scrounging cake."

"Yeah, right," she scoffed.

Royce came back and sat on the bed. He frowned at Gilly's bathrobe. "I suppose you're gonna want to put this back on."

"Fear is not my idea of an aphrodisiac."

She took the robe and slipped it on and Royce, behaving like a true southern gentleman, sat with his back to her. Well, almost, anyway.

"You know," she said, "I'd be willing to bet that little visit was a fishing expedition. He must have heard me leave my room and figured I'd come to yours. In fact, he probably came over here to see if I overheard anything he said."

"Mebbe."

"So, was that why the bedroom scene just now?" Gilly asked.

"For just in case you're right."

She smiled at him. "You really are brilliant."

"Thanks," he said, looking pleased. "I'd rather have him think you came running to my room 'cause you're hot to have me than because you wanted to spill your guts. That'll give him something to report to whoever he might be in cahoots with. If he is. Gotta say, though, I'm still havin' a hard time buyin' all this."

"I wish I wasn't selling it. Do you think your idea worked?"

Royce shrugged. "I don't know." He began gathering up the spilled cards. "But, just to be on the safe side, let's keep you here till your roommate comes back and I can lock you in with her."

"Thanks," Gilly said, feeling suddenly relieved.

Maybe, when she was younger she'd have felt confident to take on a bunch of bad guys single-handedly, but now, with a daughter to finish raising, she put a higher value her own skin. She much preferred being part of Team Gilly than going it alone as Gilly the Superhero. No superpowers, no black belt in karate and she was terrified of guns. She didn't even like scary movies. Nope, not cut out to be a superhero.

"I hate to think what might have happened to me if you hadn't been on this trip," she said.

"You'd have been bored. C'mon let's play some cards."

"What shall we play?"

He gave her a wicked grin. "How about strip poker?"

GILLY KNEW David had not only jumped to the conclusion Royce had intended but shared it freely when Ida gave her a disapproving look at breakfast the next morning.

"How'd you sleep?" he asked, nudging her as they helped themselves to rolls from the dining room buffet table.

The presence of other people gave her enough courage to treat him as a traveling companion instead of the menace he really was. "I slept fine," she said in an undervoice, "and I'd appreciate it if you'd keep my evening activities to yourself."

He smiled sweetly at her. "I wouldn't have told anybody if you'd been with me last night."

I'll bet you wouldn't have, thought Gilly. *And they'd have found my body floating in the Danube the next morning.*

She watched him at breakfast, flirting with Inge, speculating over the bargains they'd find in Vienna, and couldn't help questioning her reasoning of the night before. The last person in the world she'd expect to be a thief would be David. And part of some kind of smuggling ring? Really? Still, there was no denying what she'd heard.

Breakfast ended and everyone headed for their rooms to brush their teeth and gather up purses and sunglasses before setting off for a day in Vienna. Gilly was following the others out of the dining room when Royce grabbed her and pulled her back. "How about a good morning kiss for your lover?" he teased.

"Did you notice that Ida's treating me like I'm the Scarlet Woman?"

Royce wrapped his arms around her. "You're in disgrace this morning and you didn't even get to enjoy earnin' it."

"Virtue is its own reward," Gilly replied piously.

"Who told you that?"

"It wasn't you."

He chuckled and took a quick kiss from her, then steered her out the door. "C'mon, let's go be tourists."

Vienna was a huge city, tightly packed with seventeenth and eighteenth-century buildings, its streets choked with cars and tour busses. The Budget Adventures van wound through a maze of streets and finally found a place to park across from the Prater, Vienna's famous amusement park. Its enormous Ferris Wheel loomed in front of them like a giant monster. *No way,* thought Gilly, looking at it.

David wanted her to go on a ride with him. He tried especially hard to get her on the roller coaster, but she had a vision of herself having a freak accident and falling from one of the speeding cars, and politely refused.

As it turned out, he did go on the roller coaster – with Royce, Clint and Lisa. Gilly stayed below and watched. As the cars slowly climbed steep metal hills and plunged rapidly down the other side, she couldn't help thinking how easy it would be to engineer an accident. Europeans didn't seem to be as safety conscious as Americans. Not every ride had seat belts, a handy opportunity for a murderer. A pinch in the rear to make her jump and a quick shove to finish the job, and then later a sobbing David would say, "I told her not to stand up."

She remembered him on the Tegelberg, gasping, "A man just fell off the mountain," and an icy tingle scampered down her spine. Was she going to be the next "accident" the group witnessed.

"Roller coasters are much safer than they look," said a voice at her elbow.

She jumped and turned to see Carl standing next to her and actually smiling. Why was he being so friendly all of a sudden?

"If you'd like to go on the ride I'd be happy to go with you," he offered.

"No thanks," she managed. "I really do prefer to watch."

The string of cars coasted to a stop and the riders got off. "That was a great ride," David told her. "You should've gone."

"No thanks," she said. "I'm not into cheap thrills."

"Then how come you're hanging around with Royce instead of me?" He grinned and leaned playfully against her.

She smiled back weakly.

After a quick bite to eat (for everyone but Gilly, who'd lost her appetite), Rob was ready to show them the city. He motioned to two fringed surreys parked about twenty feet away.

The drivers, decked out in Lederhosen and feather-trimmed caps, nodded and smiled. With exclamations of delight, the group piled into the carts and took off at a trot.

While the others looked at the city's ornate buildings and monuments, Gilly watched the traffic and wondered who would get her first, David or a European motorist.

Next on their list of places to visit was St. Stephen's Cathedral. To Gilly's untrained eyes the cathedral, with its high gothic spire, looked big and overdone.

The basement was interesting if you liked wandering in musty smelling, cold catacombs, looking at coffins and windowed storerooms packed with the bones of the late sixteen hundreds' plague victims.

"There were so many corpses," Rob told them, "that the only way they could effectively bury them was to separate their bodies and stack the various parts together."

The talk of death and bones was not comforting.

"Quit worrying" whispered Royce. "I'm watching you every minute."

Quite worrying? Right. Easy for him to say.

The rest of the afternoon was free for the group to explore the Graben district, a pedestrian area jammed with shops, cafes, and restaurants. Inge towed Rob off, insisting he show her the best places to shop, and took Carl and Ed in her wake.

Gilly held her breath as David looked around for a companion. She breathed a sigh of relief when he attached himself to Ivan and Ida and disappeared with them. Now she could enjoy herself.

And enjoy herself she did, buying a bracelet for Mandy and an elaborate table runner for her friend Janet. Safety and the company of a charming man were the perfect antidote for her fears, and she was sorry when Royce consulted his watch and informed her it was almost time to meet the others.

They started back in the direction of St. Stephen's, looking in shop windows as they went. One window drew them in. Gilly's sweet tooth wouldn't allow her to pass by the candy shop. The displays were just too tempting. The pastel candies bedded in netting and shaped into corsages, the little gold bottles with the label that said Mozart Liqueur, delicate baskets decorated with ribbons and filled with truffles – they all demanded she enter and pay homage to the genius inside with her tourist money.

She splurged and bought some of the chocolate liqueur for Janet. Her friend claimed the girls were having a great time and Mandy was no trouble. But still, the kind of friendship that took your kid so you could go have a good time deserved chocolate liqueur.

Not for the first time, Gilly found herself wishing her parents were still around, especially her mom. She would have loved to have so much concentrated granddaughter time. Heck, she would have loved to have been on this trip with Gilly.

Her mom had been her confidante and her advisor when she went through her divorce, and it had been a shock when she died so suddenly. The last piece of advice that her mother had given her was, "You fell in love and made a mistake, but that doesn't mean you can't make up for it. Don't let your life shrink."

It sure wasn't shrinking now. Gilly was definitely living large, at least for her. She only hoped she could go on living.

"Gonna have a little nip when we get back to the hotel?" Royce teased, pointing to her purchase.

"It's a present."

"I think you should buy a bottle for yourself, too," he said. She looked at him questioningly and he grinned at her. "That way when we get back to the States you can have me over for dinner and serve me some."

She gave him a flirty look. "What makes you think I'm going to want anything to do with you when we get back?"

"Masculine intuition."

"There's no such thing," she scoffed.

"Sure there is," he insisted as they went out the door. "I'll show you." He stopped in the doorway. "Right now my masculine intuition tells me you're going to kiss me."

There was a lot to be said for masculine intuition, thought Gilly after they'd shared a kiss and were walking back out into the sunshine.

She smiled at him and squeezed his arm. "I think your ex was crazy to let you get away."

"Yeah? She said she must'a been crazy to marry me in the first place. I guess it ain't easy being with a musician."

"Oh, I don't know," Gilly said. "I'm finding it pretty easy."

They rejoined the group at four o'clock and began to make their way to the van. This was fine with Gilly. After spending most of the day on her feet she was ready to sit down.

"We'll go to our hotel and freshen up, then I'll bring anyone back who'd like to see Vienna's nightlife," said Rob. "Did anybody get tickets for the opera?"

"For what they were charging?" snorted Clint. "We decided we didn't want to go that bad."

Traffic was getting heavy, and the sidewalks teemed with pedestrians as they waited for the light to change, Gilly, Inge, Ed and Royce at the curb, the rest of the group and fifty Austrians crowded behind them.

Then it happened.

TEN

Gilly had just lifted up a sore foot and was rotating it when a hand shoved her ruthlessly out into the oncoming traffic.

Unable to catch her balance, she pitched forward into the street as the front of a car came screeching toward her. She opened her mouth to scream, but like in her worst nightmares, her screamer was broken.

The car swerved just as Royce and a man in a business suit jumped out after her and yanked her back onto the sidewalk. Royce pulled her into his arms, where she stood shaking, too stunned to cry. The others crowded around in concern.

"Are you alright?" asked David anxiously.

Clint bent over and scooped up her bag from the candy shop. The bottom of it was wet and torn.

"My chocolate liqueur," Gilly wailed.

"That's the least of your problems," Royce said, visibly upset. "That could of been your head."

The signal changed and people surged by, staring at them. "Are you alright, Gilly?" asked Rob.

Her legs were shaking and she wanted desperately to sit

down, but she took a deep breath and nodded. "I'm okay." Was that quivery, weak voice hers?

"Maybe it'd be a good idea if we found some place to have an early dinner and got her a drink," Royce suggested.

Rob nodded. "If no one's going to the opera tonight we really don't need to go back to the hotel to change. Does anybody object to staying in the city?"

No one objected.

"Okay then. There's a dance cafe not far from here. We'll get you some Schnaps and you'll feel better," he said to Gilly.

It was going to take more than a drink of Schnaps to make her feel better, but she nodded and followed Rob across the street.

"What happened, anyway?" David asked after they'd gotten across. "Did you lose your balance?"

Gilly looked him in the eye and said, "Yeah, with a little help. Someone pushed me."

His mouth fell open. "Pushed you! You mean on purpose?"

Gilly nodded, her eyes still locked with his.

He looked frankly disbelieving. "In a crowd like that how could you tell? Someone probably accidentally bumped into you."

Gilly knew the difference between being accidentally bumped and deliberately pushed. "Are you accident prone, David?" she asked quietly.

His face turned red and his eyes widened.

Gilly looked away, ending the conversation. Royce put a protective arm around her shoulder and led her off, leaving the stunned-looking David to follow.

The dance cafe was picturesque, complete with a small ensemble of musicians who played while the Viennese chatted over drinks of coffee, ate pastry, and danced. Gilly's hand shook when she first lifted her drink to her lips, but after a while she began to feel a little calmer.

"C'mon, let's dance," suggested Royce.

After several false starts, they gave up trying to actually dance and settled for shuffling around in one spot.

"We'd do better if you'd let me lead," she complained. "And I'm getting a crick in my neck from looking up at you."

"Almost getting killed sure makes you cranky," observed her partner.

The thought of what nearly happened made her want to cry. "It has ruined my sweet disposition," she said, trying to match his light tone. "I thought you were going to protect me."

"I saved you, didn't I?"

"Saving is not the same as protecting. You know, we're not exactly *Dancing with the Stars* pros. Can we sit down?"

"No. I asked you to dance 'cause I wanted to talk to you alone. I think you might be right. We need to try and get into David and Rob's room and see if we can find those books. This kid means business."

Gilly looked at him in irritation. "I told you that last night!"

"I know, but I found it all so damn hard to believe. I don't anymore."

She was somewhat mollified by this speech. "Well, I'm already a step ahead of you. I was going to try and get into his room yesterday when I went up to get my purse. Unfortunately, he decided to go with me. Probably to keep an eye on me."

"If that's the case, he'll start sticking to us tighter'n a tick," Royce predicted.

Gilly chewed on her lip. "We'll have to think of some way to distract him," she said at last. "We've got to search his room."

"You're right about that. Nobody would believe this farfetched fairy tale without some evidence."

It was still fairly early in the evening when the group arrived back at the hotel, and the only ones interested in going to bed were Ivan, Ida, and Carl. "How about some cards?" suggested Clint, motioning to the couches and coffee table in the small lobby.

Lisa pulled a deck of cards out of her purse and they all settled around the coffee table. But Gilly found it hard to concentrate on her cards, and after the first two hands packed it in, pleading fatigue.

"I think I must be more tired than I thought," she said. "You guys carry on without me."

Royce stood up. "I'll walk you to your room."

The other players were already absorbed in the next hand by the time they reached the elevator. "Now's our chance," he whispered. "We'll have to hurry though. I'll lay you odds our buddy will be up to check on us before ten minutes is up."

There was a comforting thought.

"How were you gonna get in yesterday?" he asked once they got off the elevator.

"I was hoping this place would turn out to be like the one we stayed at in Würselen where all the locks were the same."

Royce stopped dead in his tracks. "What? You're kiddin' me."

Gilly grabbed his arm and set him in motion again. "No, I'm not. That was how David got into Carl's room to snoop around. And that was how I ended up in there, too, because I didn't believe him." She shook her head. "To think I was hiding under the bed with a killer."

"Kinky," he teased.

At David's door they took one last look down the hall before Royce tried his key in the lock. The hotel in Krems was not like the one in Würselen. "Shit," he muttered.

"Try mine," said Gilly.

Her key wasn't any more helpful. "Now what?" she asked.

"Well, we probably don't have time to pull the old lost my room key trick. How close are the windows of your rooms?"

Gilly knew where he was going immediately and looked at him in horror. There were no friendly shrubs below to break a person's fall, only cobblestones. "Have you noticed how far down it is from this floor?"

"You got a better idea?"

Down the hall the elevator slid open, and before Gilly knew what had happened, Royce had pulled her from David's door to hers and spun her into his arms. Any protest was cut off as he clamped his lips over hers. She stared at him in amazement and the eyes looking back at her rolled in the direction of the approaching person before shutting in pretended passion.

He threaded a hand through her hair and let a convincing moan escape as David drew near. Then, as if he'd just realized there was another person present, he lifted his head in surprise.

The man should have been an actor, thought Gilly, as Royce glared at David.

"If you didn't want to be interrupted you two should've been doing that in her room, you know," David said.

"We were getting to it," said Royce. "And if I'd known we were gonna be followed I'd have already been in there."

"I wasn't following you." David sniffed and rubbed his nose. "I just came up to get a Sudafed. My allergies are acting up."

"Gimme your key," Royce said to Gilly. She handed it over and he unlocked her door. Once inside he shut it firmly behind him, scooped her up and began to carry her to the nearest bed.

"What are you doing?" she hissed.

"Sssh," he whispered. "I'm allayin' suspicion. Anyway, I thought women liked this sort of thing." He tripped over one of

Inge's shoes and they both fell onto the bed, crashing into the wall in the process.

Gilly grimaced. "Thanks. That'll give him something new to talk about at breakfast."

"Fifty Shades," he said with a grin. He motioned for her to be quiet and sat listening. A couple of minutes of silence and they could hear the door to David's room closing. "Alright," he said, jumping up. "I think we've got him convinced we're up here to mess around and not to snoop around."

"Hey, that's pretty good," said Gilly. "You really do have a way with words."

"Never mind that. Check to make sure he's gone," Royce said, moving away to grapple with the problem of the windows.

Gilly peered out the door and saw David walking off down the hall. "We're good," she said and came to stand next to Royce. "This is not a good idea." Maybe they had time to go get a key after all. Much safer than dangling from a window.

"I think these windows are close enough that I can make it."

She leaned on the sill and looked down. "No," she said firmly. "Too dangerous."

"Nah," he said. "Breakin' up a fight in a bar, that's dangerous."

"And speaking of breaking, I'm not going to stand here and watch you break your neck."

"Well, then, we'll tie something around me so I don't slip."

Gilly chewed her lip and looked around the room. All she could see was the time-honored bedsheets. It worked in books. She stripped one of the beds and brought a sheet to him.

He cocked an eyebrow. "Anybody ever tell you that you watch too many movies?"

"Working with what we've got."

He grunted and tied one end of the sheet around his waist.

Then he dragged the nearest bed against the window and tied the other end of the sheet to that. He surveyed his work and shook his head. "This ain't gonna be long enough."

Gilly took the top sheet from the other bed and handed it to him.

"I just wish I knew who his boss is," Royce said as he tied the sheets together.

"If we can find those books we can prove he's an apprentice crook and the German police can take care of figuring that out," Gilly said.

"I'll lay you odds there's been more stolen this trip than just those books," said Royce.

She nodded. "And he's been making contacts almost everywhere we went. I'm sure Van Yeck was in cahoots with him and whoever." She told Royce about Van Yeck's careless remarks in the bar, and David's mysterious visitor. "Oh!" She snapped her fingers as a new light went off in her head. "And remember that man David tried to pick up in the ice cream parlor in Oberwesel? Now, there was a criminal type if ever I've seen one."

"Have you ever seen one?"

"Only in movies," Gilly admitted. "But that man sure fit the part. Then there was the note," she continued.

"What note?"

"Someone left a note in Inge's and my room at the castle in Oberwesel. That is, our *first* room, the one we wound up in when everyone was grabbing keys. Right after I found the note David showed up. Of course, so did Ivan and Ida. Mr. Thompson can't have a room with an eastern exposure, you know," Gilly added, giving a fair imitation of Ida. "I suppose if we'd stuck around longer Carl would have put in an appearance, too."

"What did the note say?"

"I couldn't make out most of it. But it had something to do

with buying or a buyer. And, now that I think of it, the last sentence could have been a threat. It started with 'Don't'."

"Well, get it out. Let's have a look at it. Have you got one of those German-English dictionary apps on your phone? Maybe between the two of us we can figure out what..." Gilly's blush brought Royce to a stop. "You don't have it?" he guessed.

"Somebody stole it out of my purse."

"When would someone have a chance to get at your purse?"

Gilly thought, then scowled. "During my siesta on the Rhine cruise, maybe. Were you with me the whole time?"

"No," he admitted. "I went to the head, stopped to visit with Ed and Inge, and got a drink. By the time I came back, David was there."

"Hmm," said Gilly. "Clint was gone."

"He got sidetracked talking to the bartender," said Royce. "I saw him."

"If Lisa got up to go to the bathroom or something..."

"Saw her down below, too," said Royce.

"Then my purse and I were all alone."

"With David."

They looked at each other.

"That note would have told us a lot," Gilly said miserably. "It was probably from Mr. Big, himself. David must have sent him a message, giving him what he thought would be his room number."

"He wouldn't know ahead of time. More likely the guy had a messenger waiting for him. And watching."

"There's probably been somebody watching us everywhere we've gone." There was a thought to freeze a girl's blood.

"Could be," agreed Royce. "Or maybe this mail man goofed up and left the note at the room where he thought the kid would be."

"That makes sense," Gilly said. "The man David tried to talk to in the ice cream parlor! Do you think...?"

Royce shook his head. "Too obvious. But somebody's in cahoots with him, that's for sure. The kid's smart but we both know he's not capable of doing this on his own. And I've got my own suspicions about who the one in charge is."

"The logical thing to do would be to tell Rob and let him handle this," said Gilly.

"Hu-uh. That's who I suspect his boss is," said Royce, giving the knotted sheets one final tug.

"Rob?" scoffed Gilly. "He's too respectable. Besides, David drives him crazy. I think Rob's suffering extreme torture having to room with him."

Royce chuckled. "A little of David goes a long way. But remember, crime makes strange bedfellows, so the fact that he drives Rob nuts don't mean a thing."

"I think that theory's a little far-fetched. Besides, I haven't given you all the facts yet, and believe me, Ed makes a better candidate for a crook than Rob."

"Ed! You gotta be kidding."

"No, I'm not. How do we know Ed's the respectable man of leisure he pretends to be? Don't you think it's odd that he doesn't work for a living?"

"No. Why should he? He made some good investments."

"So he says, but maybe he's invested in something other than stocks. Maybe he's got a little diamond business on the side. Remember when David managed to spill those diamonds at the diamond cutters'? I saw Ed slip one into his pants pocket when the rest of us were playing pick-up. Who knows? Maybe he managed to filch several."

"Ed?" Royce was frankly disbelieving.

"I'd be willing to bet the cost of David's luggage that Ed's into something shady."

Royce rolled his eyes.

"You don't believe me. I didn't think anyone would, which is why I didn't say anything. In fact, I could hardly believe it myself. But you've got to admit it's a clever trick. One spills the diamonds, the other picks them up. It gives teamwork a whole new meaning, not to mention diversifying." Royce was rubbing his chin thoughtfully and Gilly pressed home her point. "And remember how flustered Ed was when he ran into us that night in Amsterdam? Where had he been? Only a man with something to hide would act like that."

"He was a man with something to hide, alright," said Royce. "He told me later. It was just like I said, he'd slipped out for a quickie and didn't want Inge to know."

"What a weak story," Gilly said with a snort.

"I dunno. Maybe that's something he always wanted to do. You know, something to tell the boys about when he gets back home."

"In this day and age? Why pay for it when you can get it for free?" Inge would be happy to make a donation.

Royce shrugged. "Don't know what to tell you."

"Alright," she said. "I think that's disgusting, but I'll concede it's a possibility. But that's not all I've got on Ed. How about the way he conveniently turned up missing just as that poor man was getting pushed off the Tegelberg? Inge said she couldn't find him. He probably was right there with David, helping push."

"He probably had to go to the can. And besides, half the people in the group were missing. We were scattered everywhere."

"And did you hear his comment about the books at the monastery? He knew how old they were."

"*I* knew how old they were. It's in the itinerary. Look, our fearless leader makes just as good a candidate for gangster of the year. He knows the country and the language."

"David doesn't need someone who knows the language. He can speak it," said Gilly. Well, sort of.

The expression on Royce's face said what he thought of David's German. "Naw. You gotta admit, leading a tour group makes a damned good cover for a cheap crook."

"Ed has acted a lot more suspicious than Rob," insisted Gilly.

"That's why you ought to suspect Rob. Don't you ever watch those murder mysteries on T.V.? The bad guy is always the one who's the least obvious."

"I can't believe you're comparing a T.V. show to real life."

"Art imitates life."

"Have you seen the size of the rock on Ed's dinner ring?" Gilly argued.

"Have you taken a close look at the sparkles on Rob's watch?" Royce countered.

"Alright," she said. "How about the mysterious disappearing act Ed and David did when you guys were loose in Amsterdam's red-light district?"

"They went into one of those sex shops," said Royce.

"How do you know? Were you with them?"

"No. I was with Inge," he said, an incriminating flush stealing up his neck. "But I saw them go in."

"Well, how do you know they weren't meeting some international underworld creep in there?" Gilly persisted.

"I don't. But if I remember correctly, Rob wasn't with any of us. Was he with you?"

"No."

"Then how do you know *he* wasn't with some international underworld creep?"

Gilly clamped her lips shut in irritation.

"And while we're pickin' on members of the group," said Royce, "don't forget your buddy, Carl. That note you got at the castle was in German. I'll bet he reads Deutsch real well. And he manages to give the rest of us the shake a lot. He could be off somewhere makin' deals for all we know."

"Yeah, but if Carl is Mr. Big, why isn't he still rooming with David so he can keep an eye on him?"

"After he caught David showing you his stuff? He'd be crazy to keep David in the same room with him. And anyway, wouldn't it be just like David to play those little games with him, lettin' everybody think Carl's got a secret, sneakin' you into his room?" Royce shook his head. "You gotta wonder about people, don'tcha? Why would any self-respecting crook want to take on David as a partner in crime?"

Gilly shrugged. "Maybe whoever it is took him on as a favor to someone. Anyway, you've got to admit David makes an unlikely looking crook."

"Yeah," Royce agreed. "With that fresh scrubbed, clean cut youth look and that big mouth of his he ain't my idea of a bad guy. Someone like Carl, who looks the part, would definitely need a front man. Not that I think Carl's our man." Royce hoisted himself up onto the ledge. "Right now all we're doing is guessin', so let's not say anything to anybody until we get some proof. Okay?"

"Okay," Gilly agreed. She watched him uneasily. "We'd better bag this. We've wasted a lot of time talking. David or Rob might come to the room and catch you."

"I'll be fast," he promised.

She took another peek over the windowsill. The image of a broken watermelon came to mind. What would Royce look like splattered all over the pavement? She didn't want to know.

"Don't do this," she pleaded. "You might fall."

"That's why we tied the sheets on me. I ain't gonna fall."

He stuck an exploratory foot out in the direction of the neigh-boring window. "Aw, hell," he muttered. "I'll have to jump."

"Are you nuts! Get off that ledge," ordered Gilly.

"Quit yellin' at me. I can't concentrate."

She turned her back to the window and buried her face in her hands. She heard the sound of hard breathing and feet edging along the windowsill. Now Royce was springing for the jump. She could tell without even looking. A split second later she heard the thud of feet against stone, a guttural scream, and the sound of something – correction, someone – scraping against the wall below her window on his way down.

ELEVEN

The bed jumped forward and hit Gilly in the shin. She uncovered her eyes and saw that the sheet was still connected to it and pulled taut. She whirled around and looked out the window. Royce dangled beneath her, struggling to get his feet braced against the wall. She began yanking on the sheet.

"You big twit," she puffed. "I told you not to try that!"

He was too busy grunting and scaling the wall to reply. At last he threw an arm over the window and then a leg. She grabbed him by the seat of the pants and pulled him the rest of the way in, and they both fell onto the bed, panting.

"There's nothing worse than an I told you so," he said between gasps.

She ran a shaking hand through her hair and sat back on her heels, looking at him. Then she ran grabbed him and kissed him. "Thank God you're alright."

He let out his breath and shook his head. "You're right," he said. "This window business won't work. We'll have to wait and hope we get another chance later on." He brought up a knee, and propped his elbow on it. "You know, that was pretty dumb. I think I've been watchin' too many movies, myself."

"I think we should just go to the police and tell them what we know," she said.

"I dunno," he said doubtfully. "Who's gonna believe us without evidence? After all, I didn't even believe you at first."

"I guess you're right." She sighed. "But we'll have to find a way to search his things tomorrow. I mean, he might pass the books off to someone if we don't hurry up and get them."

Royce nodded. "We'll have to get a spare key from the desk clerk and search while everybody's eatin' breakfast. You'll probably hear him leave, so come get me when the coast is clear." He began to struggle with the sheet at his waist. "We'd better get things put to rights before Inge gets back. If she comes in here and finds me tied to this bed they're really gonna have somethin' to talk about at breakfast tomorrow."

Royce's weight had pulled the knots connecting the two sheets so tightly it was impossible to disconnect them, either from each other or the bed. Gilly dug out her manicure scissors and cut the makeshift rope loose, then threw the whole mess under the bed once they'd moved it back in place.

"And you run a house cleaning service?" he cracked.

"My daughter pulls this kind of thing all the time," she said.

They heard Inge's key in the lock as they were putting the blankets back on the second bed. She sailed into the room and gave them a knowing smile. "Should I come back later?"

"No," said Royce, grinning. "We're done." He kissed the top of Gilly's head. "G'night," he murmured. "See you in the morning."

"You forgot to wish her pleasant dreams," teased Inge as he walked past her.

"No need. Her dreams have already come true," he said, putting on his thickest Southern drawl.

"You're cute," said Gilly, "but you can be replaced."

"Let me know if you decide to," Inge said, shutting the door.

"Shame on you," Gilly scolded. "I thought you and Ed had become a hot item."

Inge shrugged. "We are. But men are like cars, Schatzi. You shouldn't drive just one or it will wear out and break." She climbed into her Victoria's Secret special and pulled back the covers to her bed. "There's no top sheet!"

Gilly improvised quickly. "Mine doesn't have one, either. This hotel must put only one sheet on their beds. You know, money saving measures."

"I guess," Inge said dubiously. She climbed into bed. "Sleep well."

After what Gilly had gone through that day she figured she'd probably have nightmares.

Maybe she wouldn't. She couldn't get to sleep. She tossed and turned and reviewed her possible suspects.

Carl. He did have that list of names and addresses. Contacts, perhaps? But he hated David. They'd never work together.

Ed. He was a possibility, but he really seemed more interested in pursuing Inge than a life of crime. He was probably nothing more than an opportunist without principles. Scratch him.

Rob? He knew German, but he just didn't seem the type. And he always had people around him. When did he have time for criminal activities?

She circled back to Carl. He had plenty of time, and plenty of unaccounted absences. He had to know German with all those contacts all around the country. But if he knew so many people why hadn't he come over on his own? Why, indeed!

Unless he wanted a cover. A tour group was nice and normal. Safe. Carl was definitely a possibility.

Actually, so was Clint. What were those investments he'd made that were going to pay off so big he could quit work soon? *Oh, don't be ridiculous,* Gilly told herself. Clint was as subtle as a boulder.

Her head was beginning to throb. She knew she was no good at this sort of thing. She'd never been able to solve mysteries, either in paperback or on the screen. How could she possibly do it in real life? Heck, she wasn't even good at jigsaw puzzles. Now here she was, stuck in the middle of a jigsaw with some dangerously jagged edges.

The next morning she let Inge have first crack at the bathroom, telling herself it would make a plausible excuse for being late to breakfast.

"You're going to miss breakfast," Inge cautioned, putting the finishing touches on her make-up.

"You're right. I guess I'd better get moving," Gilly said, and stayed where she was.

Inge took one last look at herself and headed for the door, calling over her shoulder, "See you down there."

"Alright," said Gilly.

The door shut and she forced herself out of bed. She dressed in record time, listening all the while for sounds of activity from the room next door. She could hear muffled voices and people moving around, and finally she heard the door shut. She ran to her door and listened. Rob and David's voices were now in the hall. The voices grew fainter and she cracked her door and peered out. They stood at the far end the hall, waiting for the elevator. She watched them get in, then made a beeline down the hall to Royce's room and scratched on the door. .

He opened it and asked, "Is the coast clear?"

She nodded.

"Okay," he said. "Let's see if we can talk the desk clerk into giving us a room key."

They went down the hall at a brisk walk. Gilly stopped in front of the elevator but Royce motioned her to the stairs, saying, "We don't want to run into anybody we know."

They dashed down the stairs and approached the desk. Gilly took a deep breath and cleared her throat. "Entschuldigen Sie," she said. "Mein Mann hat seinen Zimmerschlüssel..." Forgot. What was the word for forgot? "Um, vergessen," she tried. "Vergessen im Zimmer."

The clerk looked sympathetic and nodded encouragingly.

"Haben Sie einen anderen?" she finished.

The clerk smiled unsuspectingly at the dumb tourists who'd locked their key in their room. "Was ist die Zimmernummer?" she asked.

"Room number?" Gilly stammered. *The one next to mine.*

"Seven-o-eight," Royce prompted and held up the appropriate fingers.

The desk clerk handed over the key and Gilly looked at it in amazement. It was so incredibly easy to be sneaky!

Royce took her arm. "C'mon dear," he said, pulling her away. "We don't want to miss breakfast, do we?" He turned to the desk clerk. "We'll bring this right back."

She merely smiled and nodded and returned her attention to her computer screen.

They hurried back to David and Rob's room. Royce made one last check down the hall, then turned the key and let them in.

Rob's side of the room was neat and orderly, his suitcase shut and ready to be loaded in the van. David's side of the room looked like slob city. A pair of jeans lay discarded on the bed. Socks and underwear littered the floor next to it. Gilly grabbed his bucket bag and opened it. All she found was a stale roll, his cell phone, breath mints and his German/English dictionary. Pretty old fashioned considering he could have simply put an app on his phone. Maybe he was using it as some sort of code book. Whatever he was using it for, it wasn't what she'd hoped to find.

"Of course," she muttered, "he wouldn't keep his treasure in there. Not after our conversation in the elevator."

Royce tried in vain to open David's suitcase and swore. "It's locked."

Gilly looked thoughtfully at the suitcase. "I've got the same kind. I wonder if my key would work." She pulled a small luggage key out of her jeans pocket and handed it to Royce.

He inserted the little key and turned it. The lock clicked. "Smart girl," he approved and Gilly smiled in satisfaction.

Yes, she was. Maybe this mystery solving stuff wasn't so hard after all.

Royce searched one section with no luck, carefully closed the dividing flap over it and turned to the other side. The stolen books weren't there, either. He slammed the suitcase shut.

"Drat," muttered Gilly. "What has he done with them?"

"Beats me. Obviously, he's not going to pack them till the last minute." Royce walked over to the desk and began rifling through drawers.

Gilly stood looking thoughtfully at David's area of the room. He probably wouldn't hide them there. She scanned the rest of the room, trying to think like David.

Well, it's worth a try, she thought. She knelt down and felt around under Rob's bed. Her hands closed around a rectangular object and she pulled out a brown paper package, neatly taped and addressed to an Erna Brown in Seattle.

"Bingo," she said, and handed it to Royce. "That's got to be them. It's the same size as the hole I saw at the monastery."

He grinned at her. "Pretty good, Sherlock." He shook his head. "Not much of a hiding place, under a bed."

"He fooled you."

Royce made no comment on that. "Let's get outta here," he said, steering her toward the door.

Back in the hall he handed her the room key. "You turn the key in and hot foot it to the dining room as fast as you can. I'm gonna stow this away in my suitcase."

Gilly nodded and ran back down the hall. She pushed the elevator button and took a deep breath to calm herself. *Nobody knows what you've been up to. There's no need to be nervous* Still, she jumped when the elevator slid open to reveal Carl and David.

"So you finally got up," David said to her.

"How are you this morning?" asked Carl. His voice held as much warmth as an ice cube.

"I'm fine," she said.

"You must be more careful," he said sternly. "You would hate to have a bad accident and spoil your vacation."

Gilly felt the blood draining from her face. What was this, a threat? "I'll be careful," she said, backing quickly away toward the stairwell. *Starting now.*

"Where are you going?" asked David.

"To breakfast," she said.

"Why don't you take the elevator?" he suggested.

"I think I'll take the stairs. I need the exercise," she called over her shoulder, and bolted downstairs.

She turned in the spare key at the desk and hurried to the dining room. David and Carl were making their way down the buffet table and the others were half finished. Her nerves were on edge and her stomach was queasy. She took a Brötchen and some tea and let it go at that.

"I'm afraid I'll have to ask you to eat fast," Rob said to the newcomers. "We'll be leaving in twenty minutes."

Twenty minutes? When would she get to the police? "No problem. I'm already packed," she lied.

"We've got a five-hour drive to Augsburg," Clint informed her. "Don't drink too much coffee."

"We'll stop and get some lunch along the way, but it will be a quick one," Rob said, rising. "Let's meet at the van at eight-thirty." The others nodded and he left, passing Royce on his way out.

Royce sauntered over to the buffet table and helped himself to a small package of corn flakes and the last two Brötchen, then came to the table and sat next to Gilly. "Did you dream about me last night?" he asked, and winked at Inge.

Gilly was too nervous to come up with a clever reply. She ignored his remark and reached for her coffee cup. Her hand was shaking as she raised it to her lips, the coffee sloshing around. She put down the cup and watched Royce reach for the milk with an incredibly steady paw. He obviously had everything under control, including himself. There was no sense in her sticking around. She'd beat it back to her room and safety, and he could stay here and keep the show going.

"I think I'll go finish packing," she said casually, rising.

"I thought you said you were done," said Lisa.

Gilly cheeks burned. "I almost am," she stuttered. "I just have a couple of things left to do." She pushed in her chair and began to walk slowly, calmly toward the door.

A chair scraped behind her and she heard Ed say, "See you all at the van."

Gilly picked up her pace, counting the steps to the door. Next to David and Carl, there was no one with whom she'd less rather have a cozy chat. She gained the door and trotted – calmly – for the stairs. If she could just get part way up them she'd be safe. Ed would never even attempt to make it up all those flights.

"Gilly," called a hearty voice behind her. "No sense taking the stairs when the elevator's right here."

"Oh, I need the exercise."

"We'll get plenty of that walking around Augsburg," Ed assured her. He stood, holding the door open, waiting for her to join him.

She took her foot off the bottom step and walked toward the elevator, feeling like a fly with one foot in a web. He was retired, he was harmless. Royce had said so.

What did Royce know? She entered the elevator, smiled weakly at Ed and placed herself against the far wall.

He asked her how she was feeling.

"Fine," she squeaked.

"You had a nasty scare yesterday," he said. "You got to be careful traveling in these foreign countries. You never know what could happen to you."

Kind advice or sinister threat? Hadn't she just heard the same thing from Carl? Who was being kind and who was trying to scare her? Gilly nodded and swallowed hard.

"I had an aunt," Ed continued. "She was a nosy old biddy. Thought she saw someone shoplifting in a jewelry shop once. Tried to make a citizen's arrest. Went chasing these punks out into the street, not watching where she was going, and got mowed down by taxi driver." Ed shook his head. "These people over here drive like maniacs. You never know when one could be gunning for you."

The back of Gilly's neck turned prickly and hot and river of sweat began wending its way toward middle of her bra. She managed a weak nod.

"Here we are," he announced cheerfully.

The door opened and he held it for her. She scuttled out and sped for the safety of her room.

Once inside it, she realized she was breathing as if she'd just run five miles and her legs were shaking. She collapsed on her bed and sat staring at her trembling hands. Everyone was out to get her. She wished she was home. No. She wished she was in high school again with no worries. No, wait. She'd had zits then and had trouble getting a date till her junior year. Okay, she wished she was in grade school. Forget that. She wished she was back in the womb. She grabbed her pillow and curled herself around it.

The sound of Inge's key in the lock shocked her out of her reverie. She looked at the pillow in disgust and threw it from her, got up and began stuffing the last of her things in her suitcase.

Nothing's going to happen to you, she told herself sternly. *Get a grip!*

Had David looked under his bed yet? What would happen when he did and found the books gone? The answer to that was easy. He'd come after the woman who knew too much.

That was it. She was going to the police. Now.

TWELVE

"I'll be right back," Gilly told Inge and hurried down the hall. She met Royce and Ed coming from the other direction.

"All ready to go?" asked Ed.

"Yes, and I think Inge could use some help with her luggage," Gilly told him.

"I'll go help her," he said in a take charge voice and strutted away.

As soon as Gilly thought he was out of range she hissed, "We need to go to the police. Now. Before we leave."

"There ain't time. We're leavin' town in a few minutes."

"We're also leaving the country. If we don't go now, it will be too late."

"It won't be too late. They'll be just as glad to get back stolen property in Germany as they will in Austria. Believe me."

"But it's crazy to wait," Gilly said, her voice rising. "Let's get this all tied up now, while we've got the evidence and I'm still alive."

He looked over his shoulder, then drew her further down

the hall. "Not so loud."

"Give me one good reason why we shouldn't go to the police right now," she hissed.

"Because David didn't take those books."

Gilly looked at him blankly. "What are you talking about?"

"I was thinkin' all last night about our conversation yesterday, and somethin' didn't set right. Then at breakfast it came to me." He looked down the hall once more before continuing. "Remember how we said David makes an unlikely lookin' crook. Well, I think that's because he ain't one. And he ain't a front man. He's a fall guy."

"How do you know that?"

"I don't. But I'm ninety-nine percent sure of it."

"What is this, your male intuition again?" Which was all well and good for predicting kisses but probably not up for ferreting out arch villains.

"Somethin' like that. And if we go to the cops before we've had a chance to sort this out a little better you can bet David will take the rap for something he didn't do."

Voices down the hall made both Gilly and Royce start. "Come on, Schatzi," caroled Inge. "We've got to go."

Gilly started down the hall and Royce grabbed her arm. "Don't say anything. Not yet."

"Shit," she muttered.

BY EIGHT-THIRTY THE van was on its way. They would be circling back into Germany for the final leg of the tour, their first destination the medieval city of Augsburg. Gilly had observed David carefully while they were loading up and had come to the conclusion that he was either a great actor or Royce was right.

Still, they shouldn't be the ones trying to sort this all out. They weren't police or private detectives. They were a couple of average people who had no idea how to handle dangerous situations. The longer they held onto those books, the greater the chances were that one or both of them would soon be having an "accident" similar to the one Gilly had in Vienna.

She'd give Royce one day to figure this thing out. One day. If he hadn't come up with something by the next day they were going to the cops. Playing cat and mouse with a killer was crazy.

Killer! How could Royce have forgotten that cute little conversation she'd overheard where David promised to take care of her? Even dumber, how could she have forgotten it? That proved Royce's theory was nuts.

She pulled out her itinerary and consulted it. The next day was Landsberg. They were scheduled to visit the prison where Hitler wrote *Mein Kompf* and, wunderbar, the afternoon was free. She and Royce could slip away to the nearest police station, give them the evidence and let them tow David away. He'd spill his guts and they'd cart off his partner in crime, whoever he was, and Gilly could tour happily ever after.

Just get through this day, she told herself. After tomorrow it would be all over, whether Royce Sherlock Clark had things figured out or not.

The morning's drive was uneventful. Gilly did have some moments of terror as they approached the German border. Were the authorities searching for those missing books? If they were stopped and searched how would Royce explain to the border guard what he was doing in possession of them?

But they encountered not problem going from one country to another. A tour group seemed to make the perfect cover for a thief.

They encountered some delays on the way to Augsburg.

Slow service at a roadside Gasthaus put them behind schedule, but what really threw Rob's well-planned day into a spin was David managing to get sick in the van shortly after they hit the road.

Ida, who had been unusually quiet all morning came to life when the need for a mother arose, producing Pepto-Bismol tablets from her purse and instructing David to take two. To Rob, she suggested he find a gas station where he could clean the van properly.

"I'm sure you could use the practice cleaning up messes," she said, and Rob's face turned pink. Gilly and Inge exchanged glances and both offered to help their embarrassed leader.

Poor Rob, thought Gilly. He was doing his best. And anyway, some of the things that had gone wrong on the tour hadn't even been his fault. Ida surely couldn't blame him for their delay on the Tegelberg, or the room mix-up in Oberwesel. And she certainly couldn't blame him for David getting sick. Some things were simply out of a man's control.

Clean-up took a while and when they finally got to Augsburg, Rob's flock of tourists had turned into Carl clones, silent and frowning.

"Thank God we're finally here," Inge said as they got out of the van.

Amen to that, Gilly thought. In spite of Rob's cleaning efforts and riding with the windows down, the van had carried a smell that was almost enough to make her want to barf.

And stress and worry had left her exhausted. Where was an energy drink when you needed one?

She looked around her room, complete with shower and toilet and flopped gratefully on the nearest bed. "All the comforts of home," she sighed. "I'm not leaving."

"Don't lie down, Schatzi. You won't want to get up," Inge cautioned, heading for the bathroom.

"It's too late. I'm down. Just order me a Schnitzel and bring it back in a wiener-doggie bag."

"You can rest when you get back home," Inge called. "Why would you want to spend your vacation alone in a hotel room when you could be out enjoying the sights?"

Alone? The word revived Gilly instantly. If there was one thing she didn't want to be, it was alone. And vulnerable. She bolted up off the bed and joined Inge at the sink.

They got to the dining room to find everyone there except Rob and Carl. "Rob's showering," David explained. "He said not to wait for him."

"You don't have to twist my arm," said Clint.

"We've noticed," David sneered and Clint glared at him.

"Maybe you'd better go light," Ida advised David. "Give your poor stomach a chance to rest."

David's stomach, however, seemed to have recovered. He was back to normal, cracking jokes and insisting on ordering in his atrocious German.

Gilly found his chipper air unnerving. He was probably biding his time, waiting for an opportunity to steal the books back and arrange another accident for her. Well, he was out of luck. By the next day they'd be with the Landsberg police.

Rob finally joined them for dinner, and Gilly decided the shower must have washed away the day's stresses, because he looked relaxed again.

After dinner the group caught the trolley and made their way to Augsburg's open-air theatre, which was nestled in the city's huge park. The theatre was already filling with culture lovers anxious to heart Mozart's *Marriage of Figaro*, and Rob got their tickets and settled them in two rows toward the back.

The orchestra began the overture. Gilly cuddled up to Royce and prepared to enjoy herself. The books were safely squirreled away, and tomorrow they'd go to the police and this would all be over. Meanwhile, no one could do anything to her here, surrounded by all these people. She could relax.

As the second act progressed, she realized she wasn't really enjoying herself. It wasn't that she didn't appreciate any of the music. It was just that she didn't appreciate most of it. Maybe it took training to turn a person into an opera lover.

Obviously, Royce didn't have the proper training, either. His chin had fallen on his chest and he was beginning to snore. Gilly looked around to see how the other would-be culture lovers were faring. Ivan and Ida were doing fine. Ida, especially, was paying rapt attention to the movements of the costumed singers. Lisa's attention was also riveted. Clint was nodding off. And Ed and Inge were holding hands, smiling at each other, and stealing kisses. Gilly looked back over her shoulder, wondering how David was faring. His seat was empty. Where was he?

Ten minutes later she stole another look. His seat still stood empty. Another five minutes passed and still no David. What was that little crook up to now?

As the second act closed she looked and found him back in his seat, applauding enthusiastically. "What happened to you?" she asked as the group stood visiting during intermission.

He looked at her in fake wide-eyed innocence. "What do you mean?"

"You were gone for most of the second act," she informed him.

"Couldn't you find the men's' room?" taunted Clint.

"I found it," said David. "But one of the toilets in the men's' side was broken and the bathroom was flooded. So I snuck into the girls' side and then these women came in, and I wasn't about to come jumping out of the stall and yell, 'Surprise!' so I had to hide until they left."

"For the whole second act?"

"More women came in. What could I do?"

"Go in the bushes," suggested Clint.

"Gross," said David.

Figaro finally managed to get married, and by the time the group got to their hotel Gilly's bed was looking even more inviting than it had earlier. But she still hadn't had a chance to talk to Royce. She was trying to come up with a plausible excuse for leaving the room when someone knocked on the door. She opened it and there he stood. The mind reader.

"I can't sleep," he drawled. "I thought you might want to take a late-night stroll."

"I'd love one," she said. She picked up her room key and followed him out into the hall. "I was just about to come looking for you."

"We need to talk," he said and steered her down the hall.

The sober look on his face coupled with their rapid speed told her they had troubles. "What's wrong?"

"Wait until we get outside," he cautioned.

As soon as they were on the street she said, "Look, you probably think you've got this all figured out, but we can't take any chances. We have to go to the police. Tomorrow."

"Gilly," he began.

"I know what you said," she continued. "And your theories were great. But I think you were wrong about David. And – "

He cut her off. "We can't go to the police. We don't have the evidence anymore."

She'd heard wrong, right? "What?"

"I got back to my room and found the lock on my suitcase broken."

"Oh, no. Don't tell me..."

"I just did. The books are gone."

THIRTEEN

Gilly stared at Royce in disbelief. "Gone?"

"Gone."

"No. How could they be?"

"How do you think? Somebody got into my room."

"Did you lock it?"

He scowled at her. "Of course I did."

"Then how could they get in?" she demanded. That was it. She was going to have a nervous breakdown right there on the street.

"Seriously? How'd we get into Rob and David's room? The old lost key routine probably."

This couldn't be happening. Gilly stared at Royce for a moment, then burst into tears. "That little weasel!" she raged. "I'll kill him. What am I saying? He's going to kill me!" She began to laugh hysterically.

"Hey, keep it down," he said. "The whole street can hear you."

She leaned against a building. "I can't take this anymore. Let's just go to the police."

"Without proof? I speak no German. You speak a little."
He shook his head. "That ain't gonna work. We'll just have to
get the package back."

Gilly rubbed her aching head. "That should be interesting.
I don't think David's going to put the books under a bed for us
again."

"No. He's either going to pass them off to someone, say his
partner, or he's going to keep them on him."

Gilly frowned. "So much for your David-the-fall-guy
theory."

He gave her a shrug and a helpless look. "Guess I was
wrong."

She rubbed her aching forehead. "Oh, well. Back to square
one. Where would he keep the package until he could get rid
of it?"

"Someplace close to him."

"Like in his bag," she said with a knowing nod.

"Probably. We still don't know who or where his partner is,
but I doubt he'll have a chance to get rid of the books before
tomorrow. And I'm still votin' for Rob. We're just lucky there's
been no chance for either of 'em to slip away to a post office so
far. But we drove up the stakes when we took those books.
We'll have to grab 'em back tomorrow or we'll be S.O.L."

"Let's hope we don't hit town until after the post office clos-
es," Gilly added miserably.

Royce grunted in agreement. "You know what puzzles me?
When did he get a chance to search our rooms?"

"You mean your room," she corrected.

"I mean *our* rooms. I'll lay you odds that if you check carefully you'll find your things have been searched. Of course,
when he couldn't find the books there I was the next likely
subject. So he got into my room."

"He asked for keys for two different rooms?"

"I dunno. But I'm sure your stuff got searched, too. I hope he was smart enough to use his luggage key on your lock. He just busted mine." Gilly looked sympathetic, but Royce didn't notice. He was deep in thought. "I'll be hanged if I can figure when he had a chance to go through our things. We were all together like peas in a pod the whole day."

"The opera!" declared Gilly. "He was gone most of the second act. Boy, I should have suspected he was up to something rotten. Remember when I asked him during intermission what happened to him? That crazy tale about the men's' bathroom being flooded and how he got stuck in the women's' side! It all sounded so plausible when he was telling it." She ran a hand through her hair. "The boy is a monster, a real criminal genius. Can you imagine what he'll be doing in ten years?"

"Kinda blows your mind, huh?" agreed Royce. "Well, let's get back and try to get some sleep." He put an arm around her and they started down the street.

"Not even a sleeping pill could knock me out now," she said miserably.

Royce stopped. "Hey, there's an idea. Why don't you hot foot it down to Ida's room when we get back and see if she's got any sleepin' pills in that arsenal of hers? We're bound to go out tomorrow night and maybe we'll get a chance to slip one to our buddy. If we get him zonked good enough he'll fall asleep early and you can decoy Rob while I slip into their room and get the books."

"Good idea," said Gilly. "But don't you think this is getting a little complicated? Why not just tell Rob and get him to let us in the room when David's out? Or better yet, ask him to help us and look through David's things when he's in the shower?"

"Cause I don't want to ask anybody to help us. We're playin' a rough game here and we still don't know all the players. And you know what I think about him. Anyway, I don't trust a man who's too quiet."

"That's ridiculous," Gilly scoffed.

"Mebbe."

"I wish you'd stop picking on poor Rob. I think he's perfectly trustworthy."

"And nice looking?"

Gilly's cheeks heated up. "Well, yes. But..."

"And interesting?"

"What's that got to do with it?"

Royce raised an eyebrow and Gilly's chin came up. "Look," he said. "I ain't tryin' to insult you. But you like this guy. You're prepared to think he's nice just because you like him."

"You've got it all backwards," Gilly insisted. "I like him because I think he's nice."

Royce didn't look convinced and she blushed. "There," he said. "When you start thinkin' about it honestly you have to admit I'm right."

"No," she said. "It's just that you've sowed seeds of doubt in my mind and now I'm confused."

"Well, when you're confused it's better not to trust anyone."

"Oh, I guess," she said. "I'm so tired I can't think straight anymore."

"C'mon. Let's get to bed. By way of Ida's room," he added.

"Frankly, I think drugging David is too nice," she said. "I'd rather hit him on the head."

Royce grinned. "If he attaches himself to us we'll lure him into an alley, whack him on the bean and go to the police with our evidence."

The hotel hall was deserted when they went back in and Gilly looked at the Thompson's door and wondered how she'd gotten nominated for the role of scrounge. She knew they liked to turn in early and she hated bothering them. They were probably already asleep.

Well, when this was all over she'd tell Ida she'd helped stop an international thief. Then maybe the woman would forgive Gilly for waking her up.

Royce was watching her from down the hall, so she forced herself to lift her hand and knock timidly. There was no answer and she shrugged at him. He motioned for her to try again and she bit her lip and knocked once more.

"Who's there?" called a muffled voice.

"It's me, Gilly."

A minute later Ida answered the door, clad in a bathrobe that looked about as worn as her yellow sweater.

"I'm sorry to bother you," Gilly said. "Did I wake you."

Ida heaved a sigh. "What's wrong, dear?"

"I can't sleep. I was hoping you might have brought along something for that since you're so well organized." A little flattery never hurt.

Ida had been looking a little put out. Now she smiled. "As a matter of fact, I do have something." She stepped aside and motioned Gilly in. "Mr. Thompson has trouble sleeping sometimes," she said, keeping her voice low.

Gilly looked at the snoring lump in the bed. She found it hard to picture Ivan as an insomniac, but she nodded politely.

Ida rummaged in a little black toilet bag and came back with a couple of pills. "I hope this will help." She gave Gilly a motherly pat. "You're probably worried about those books. That's why you can't sleep. You need to relax and enjoy the rest of your vacation. Life's too short to spend it thinking about other people's problems."

"Thanks," said Gilly. "I'm sure the books will be found soon." She forced a smile for Ida, who gave her one back and said, "Sorry I woke you."

"It's okay," Ida said, and shut the door.

Gilly's guardian angel was still standing watch and she nodded at him. He nodded back and she padded across the hall to her room, unlocked the door and blew him a kiss. He waved and disappeared into his room.

Gilly smiled. He was doing a good job of protecting her.

Inge was already in bed and snoring. Gilly dropped the sleeping pills in a small zippered compartment in her purse, then opened her suitcase. Royce's words came back to her as she stared at its rumpled contents. David had searched her things, and he'd made no effort to hide the fact that he'd done it. The tops and shorts that had been neatly folded were now crumpled and jumbled.

Gilly swore and grabbed a wrinkled pair of shorts. *I won't be at all sorry when they pack him off to jail,* she thought as she began refolding her clothes.

The next day they hit Landsberg. Fortunately, they didn't hit it on schedule. They had a flat tire in the middle of nowhere only to discover the spare was equally flat.

Most of the Budget Adventurers rolled with this latest punch. Ida, however, was disgusted, and quick to inform Rob that he should have checked the spare when he first picked up the van. Her mood barely improved when they were rescued by a local farmer, who drove Rob somewhere to get the tires fixed. The man's wife took them in and fed them coffee and Kuchen, but even cake didn't sweeten her up much, which was surprising considering how even tempered she normally was.

"Honestly," she muttered to her husband as they sat in the small living room. "There's no excuse for such ill preparation."

Gilly supposed anyone organized enough to carry a minimarket worth of stuff in her purse would have a hard time understanding how a seasoned tour group leader could make such a rookie mistake. The rest of the gang was happy enough, and Gilly had to admit that seeing something of the everyday life of the German people was just as interesting as hitting the tourist attractions.

The setback stressed Rob though, and when they finally pulled into Landsburg late toward evening he wore a very forced smile.

"All the shops are closing," Lisa mourned.

"Everything's closing," Ida said, looking accusingly at Rob, who pressed his lips tightly together.

"We can still check out the night life," said Clint. "Let's go get something to eat."

Rob led them to a little restaurant which Inge pronounced perfect. "It has wonderful atmosphere!" she declared, looking around at the well-worn wooden booths and tables and dirndl clad waitresses. They found a table and settled in for the night, Gilly nervously fingering her purse as she slid in between Royce and David.

How was she ever going to get a chance to slip him a sleeping pill, especially with Ida along?

As it turned out, David gave her a perfect opportunity. He had been sniffing, and now he pulled out a Kleenex and blew his nose loudly.

"Got a cold?" asked Clint.

"No," sniffed David. "It's just my allergies acting up."

Ida had gone to the restroom. Opportunity was knocking. Gilly slipped a hand in her purse and pulled out the pills she'd gotten. "Here," she said. "I've got a couple of allergy pills left."

David looked at her offering but made no move to take it. "That's okay," he said. "I took something right before we came here. It should start working any minute. Besides, it's not good to take other people's medicine. You could accidentally poison yourself."

Gilly felt a guilty flush steal up her neck. *Fool*, she thought.

What made you think he'd be stupid enough to take anything from you?

"Well, I never worry about those things," said Inge. She snatched a pill from Gilly's open palm. "I could use something. My sinuses have started acting up and I've run out of my medicine."

"Wait," protested Gilly. "Didn't you just hear what David said?"

"Don't be silly, Schatsi," said Inge. "How can your allergy medicine hurt me?" At that moment their waitress appeared, her arms filled with several big steins of beer. Inge grabbed hers, popped the pill in her mouth and washed it down with a hearty swig.

"You know, you're not supposed to drink and take medicine at the same time," cautioned Gilly.

Inge looked at her like she'd gone crazy. "One beer won't hurt me."

Gilly stole a look at Royce. He sat unconcernedly guzzling beer. She took a deep drag from hers and wondered how this fiasco was going to end.

For the rest of the hour she carefully observed her fellow tablemates, trying to weed villain from suspect. Carl drank his beer, smoked his pipe, then politely wished the others a good night and excused himself. Ample proof in Gilly's eyes that he wasn't the mastermind for this caper. If he was involved, he'd have stayed to keep an eye on David, she reasoned, or rather, the books. Ed, on the other hand, showed no signs of going anywhere. Of course, neither did anyone else. Hmm.

As the meal went on, the conversation at their table became increasingly more raucous with each new round of beer, but Gilly noticed that Inge was getting quiet. Her eyelids began to droop. She finally propped an elbow on the table and cupped her chin in her hand. The hand began to slide, pulling the skin on Inge's cheek up to her eyebrow. Her head dropped to her arm and finally rolled onto her plate of Bratwurst. Ed looked at his snoring lady friend in amazement.

"I guess it's a good thing I didn't take that allergy pill, huh?" David said to Gilly.

Ida was looking at her funny, and Gilly again felt a betraying warmth on her face. She smiled weakly and said, "I told her not to drink that beer."

"I'd better get her back to her room," Ed decided.

"Let someone help you," Lisa advised him.

"It's not that far," he said. "We'll be fine."

"I'll help you," Rob said, standing up. The two men pulled Inge from the table and each hoisted an arm over their shoulders.

"Are you coming back?" called Clint, as Rob and Ed dragged the drooping Inge away.

"Keep my beer warm," Rob called back over his shoulder.

"I guess she'll sleep good tonight," said Clint. "Those allergy pills can sure knock you out."

David had been making eyes at a cute little waitress all evening. Like before, he'd gotten Rob to ask what time she got off work. This time, he'd received an encouraging reply in halting English that she would be off at nine. David had offered to see her home and she'd accepted. Now he saw her taking off her apron and looked at his watch. "Nine o'clock. I have to go be gallant," he announced, picking up his bucket bag.

"You do know what to do with a girl, right?" Clint mocked.

"Of course. You probably don't remember," David shot back.

"Why don't you leave that here," offered Ida. "We'll take it back to the hotel for you."

"That's okay," said David. "I can take it with me."

Royce took a swig of beer and watched him walk across the

room. He dug a pen out of his shirt pocket, picked up a napkin and wrote on it. "Whaddya think about this for a song title?" he asked, shoving the napkin over to Gilly.

Ida leaned over and looked at the napkin. "I'll follow him," she read. "You're probably too young to know, but that's been done before in a song." She began to sing the chorus to "I Will Follow Him."

"Yeah, I guess you're right," said Royce. "Well, how about this?" He looked at Gilly. "Somethin' like... Will you follow me?"

Gilly nodded. "Good idea."

"I guess," said Clint doubtfully. "But I gotta tell you, it doesn't do much for me."

"Yeah, I guess not," Royce said, watching David and the girl disappear through the door. "I think I'll go find the can."

"I hate to say it," said Clint after he left. "But I don't know how he ever sold a song."

"You know what they say," said Gilly. "You've got to write a lot of garbage to find a hit. She scooted off the bench. "The guys might need some help with Inge. When Royce comes back tell him I'm on my way back to the hotel."

"Hey, should you be out by yourself?" Clint objected.

"It's not far," said Gilly. "I'll be fine." Then she made a bolt for the door before Clint could turn chivalrous and escort her.

She stepped outside but saw no one in sight. Which way had David gone?

Just then a woman screamed.

FOURTEEN

Gilly ran around the corner of the building and found David lying inert on the ground, Royce standing over him. "My God," she gasped. "You killed him!"

"Naw, I just cracked him on the skull. Here. Hand me that satchel and take an arm. We gotta get outta here. That little waitress he was kissin' when I hit him screamed bloody murder and beat feet down the alley. Somebody could'a heard her."

"Somebody did, alright," said Gilly, bending to take an arm. "Me."

They hoisted the unconscious David up, dragged him out of the side street and began to make their way back to the hotel. After a block Gilly was panting heavily and her heart beating so furiously she felt sure it was going to explode. "Can we stop for just a second?" she gasped.

Royce stopped. "Here," he said, handing her the satchel. "Let's see if he's got what we need."

Gilly unzipped it and rummaged around. With a triumphant smile she brought out a familiar brown package.

She quickly stuffed it in her purse. "I knew I brought this monster along for a reason. Tomorrow we're going to the police as soon as we hit Oberammergau. I don't care what Rob has planned."

"Good idea," Royce grunted as he picked up David and slung him over his shoulder. "Now let's get Sleeping Beauty back to his room before he wakes up."

"Wait!" The command from down the street stopped them in their tracks and they turned to see Ivan and Ida trotting toward them.

"Oh, dear. What happened?" panted Ida.

Before Royce could answer they heard a hoarse command to wait and saw Clint and Lisa running up the street.

"Well, now we're all here," said Royce.

"What happened?" Clint asked.

"Somebody mugged David," Royce told him.

"You see," said Ida, shaking a finger at Gilly. "That's why Clint didn't want you to walk back to the hotel alone."

"Yeah," agreed Clint. "That could have been you."

"Did you guys all leave on account of me? You shouldn't have," Gilly said.

"We didn't think it was a good idea for you to be wandering the streets alone in a foreign country," said Ida.

Clint turned to Royce. "Need some help with him?"

"Naw, I got him," said Royce. He started moving down the street, and the others followed like a small parade.

"Did you see who did this?" asked Lisa.

"Just got a glimpse of somebody running off down the alley," Royce lied, smooth as silk. "He's probably long gone by now."

"Was anything stolen?" Clint asked.

"I don't think the guy had time. But it's a good thing I heard that little girl David was with scream and got out here when I did," Royce said.

"How did you manage to hear him from inside the restaurant?" Ida asked.

"The window in the men's room was open," said Royce. The man certainly could think fast.

"He's lucky to escape with only a bump on his head," said Lisa.

You're right, thought Gilly. *I'd love to give him several.*

"Should we call a doctor?" asked Lisa.

"He'll be okay," said Clint.

"But we'd better get some ice on it," put in Ida.

They were in the hotel now, and the pressure was beginning to get to Gilly. She felt like a stretched rubber band by the time they reached the elevator. The door slid open to reveal Rob and Ed, returning from settling Inge, and she let out a shriek.

"I think my ear drum's broken," Clint said, frowning.

"Sorry," she said. "I guess I'm a little jumpy."

"What happened?" asked Rob as the new arrivals squeezed into the elevator with them. He watched wide-eyed as Royce put David down and propped him against the wall and pressed the button for the next floor.

"David got himself mugged," said Cint.

"Is he alright? Was anything stolen from him?" Rob asked, reaching out to help hold David upright.

The door slid shut, leaving them all riding back up together. Gilly swallowed hard. The books in her purse felt like lit dynamite.

"I don't think the guy had time to take anything," Royce said. "We got there pretty quick. But you might want to check when we get him to the room and make sure his wallet ain't missin'."

The elevator stopped and Gilly was the first one off. "If you can manage without me I'm going to bed."

"We'll be fine," Royce assured her.

She made a bolt for her room, fumbling in her purse for her room key. *Just let me get inside my safe little room.*

The sound of footsteps behind her made her clumsy and the elusive key kept evading her fingers. She made one last desperate dig for it and managed to lose her grip on her purse. It fell to the floor with a thud, a corner of the brown paper package sliding out.

"Let me help you," offered Ed, bending down.

Aack! What was he doing there? Oh, yeah. Room down the hall.

Gilly quickly scooped up the purse, stuffing the package of books back inside, and took the lipstick and pencil he handed her, telling her heart to slow down. "Thanks," she managed. She looked up to find him studying her intently. Face on fire, she stood up and once again dug into her purse in search of her room key. Her trembling fingers finally closed around it and she dredged it out only to drop it.

Ed bent and picked it up. "You seem a little nervous tonight." He opened the door and handed the key back to her. "Are you okay? If you're nervous I could stay with you."

"No!" Gilly realized she was shouting. She tried for a calmer voice. "I think I just need some sleep. Goodnight," she said and shut the door in his face.

She locked it and leaned against it, breathing heavily. Why had Ed studied her so intently? It couldn't have been out of simple concern.

Inge let out a loud snore and Gilly glowered at her. Nice someone was able to sleep. Nice that someone had no clue what was going on.

A sudden cold thought grabbed Gilly's heart and gave it a

painful squeeze. Where was Inge's room key? Gilly raced to the dresser where her roommate's purse sat and dumped out its contents, searching frantically for Inge's key. She found everything from safety pins to nail files, but no room key. Maybe Ed had slipped it in his pocket when he brought her back. If he was in on all this, if he had pilfered Inge's key somehow a locked door wouldn't do any good.

Now Gilly's heart began thumping wildly. What was she going to do? What could she do? It was just her against a master criminal. She dragged a chair across the room and wedged its back under the doorknob.

Inge never stirred during her roommate's feverish activity. Gilly eyed her jealously, wishing she could sleep.

But sleep was no longer an option. Someone had to keep a watch over them. Them? No. *Only me*, Gilly thought bitterly. *Ed won't want to croak Inge. He'll keep her for himself. The only one anybody wants to get rid of is me.*

Gilly's mouth set in determined lines. Well, nobody was going to get her. She sat on her bed, her back propped against the wall, her eyes on the door. The only advantage her attacker had was the element of surprise and she'd taken that away from him. She'd wait him out, and at the first rattle of the doorknob she'd scream. Then she'd throw a lamp at him.

She sat for a while watching Inge sleep. As she became increasingly more tired her attitude of selfless denial began to deteriorate. Inge let out a particularly loud snore, and, in a burst of immaturity, Gilly took her pillow and flung it at Inge, hitting her squarely on the head. Inge let out a snort and giggled in her sleep.

"I can just imagine what you're dreaming about," Gilly muttered.

Inge burrowed deeper into her pillow and sighed happily.

Gilly turned her attention back to the door and let out a

sigh of self-pity. She could have gone for a cup of coffee right now, just for something to drink, and to help her think, not because she needed it to stay awake. She was too keyed up to fall asleep tonight. Too keyed up... too... keyed....

Soon the gentle sound of dueling snores filled the room.

FIFTEEN

A loud banging reached down into Gilly's mind and began pulling her up from the warm, dark depths. "No, don't wake up," something inside her whispered. "It's safer here." But the banging persisted. She opened one eye. "Wha..." she mumbled groggily.

"Wake up," someone called and banged again.

Inge moaned and stirred, leaving Gilly to force herself from her bed and go drag the chair away from the door. But first. "Who's there?" she asked cautiously.

"It's me," drawled a familiar voice.

She opened the door a few inches and peeked out and Royce peeked in.

"Good, you're dressed," he said.

Not such a big accomplishment considering the fact that she never got undressed. She didn't share that information as she let him in. Nobody but her needed to know she was still wearing the same underwear she'd had on the day before. Yuck.

"It's eight-thirty," he said. "Everyone's already down at

breakfast. They sent me to fetch you two. Rob wants to leave in half an hour."

"Half an hour? I thought we didn't have that far to go. Why are we leaving so early?"

"Our fearless leader wants us to see that other castle we missed the day we got stuck up on the Tegelberg, so we're gonna go there and then double back to Oberammergau."

"Shit," Gilly muttered.

"I know what you're thinkin' but don't worry. We'll get to the cops today." He gave her a quick kiss, then pointed to Inge's inert figure. "You girls will never make breakfast. You'll be lucky if you can even get her awake in half an hour."

Gilly wasn't sure she had much of an appetite anyway.

"I'll save you each a roll and some cheese," he promised, heading for the door."

"Great. How about bringing us a couple of cups of coffee on your way back?"

"You got it. By the way, keep your door locked and don't let in anybody but me."

"Already a step ahead of you there," she murmured.

She washed up and changed, then, with an effort, turned her attention to her roommate. "C'mon Inge," she said, pulling back the covers. "We're leaving in half an hour. You've got to get up. Inge!" She grabbed Inge's shoulder and shook it.

"I'm sleepy," Inge moaned.

"You shouldn't be. You've been sleeping the sleep of the dead." Dead? Gilly gulped and told herself not to go there. She took Inge's arm and pulled. "Come on. Get up."

Inge groaned and sat up only to fall back onto the bed.

"Oh, no you don't," Gilly said, pulling again. "We have to get going. Rob has a lot planned for us today."

And so did Gilly. The sooner they got to Oberammergau and the police the better she'd like it.

"Okay, okay," groaned Inge, staggering to her feet. "What time is it, anyway?"

"You don't want to know. I can tell you this much. You've got about fifteen minutes to get gorgeous, so make it a rush job."

"What?" squeaked Inge. "Fifteen minutes! It takes me that long just to put on my makeup."

"Well, you'd better plan on only wearing half your paint today, because that's all the time we've got."

Inge hit warp speed and began gathering and pulling on her clothes. She stopped suddenly, staring at her spilled purse in irritation. "What's this?"

"I did that," Gilly confessed. "Sorry. I was looking for your room key."

Inge bent down and picked a shiny brass object from the floor and held it up.

Gilly's eyes widened. "It was there all the time," she said. "I lost a night's sleep for nothing. It must have fallen out of your purse when they brought you up."

"What are you talking about?" Inge demanded. "Why did you want my key?"

Gilly shook her head. "Never mind."

"How can I never mind when you're acting so strange?"

Gilly shook her head. "It's too long a story, and we've got about eight minutes left."

Inge gave up the interrogation, muttering as she grabbed her makeup bag.

Five minutes later there was a knock at the door. "Room service," called Royce.

"Great," said Gilly. "Coffee."

"Thank God," Inge murmured, not stopping her face work.

Gilly opened the door and Royce came in, balancing two napkin encased bundles and two cups of coffee. He handed a cup to Gilly. "Black, right?"

She nodded. "Thanks. I definitely needed something to wake me up."

"I guess," said Royce. "Both you girls were dead to the world. I must'a stood knockin' for ten minutes."

"I've never had an allergy pill affect me like that," said Inge. "It would make a great sleeping pill."

Gilly choked on her coffee.

"You about ready?" asked Royce. "Everybody's gathering up their gear and going down to the van."

Inge shut her lipstick and examined her face in the mirror. "It will have to do."

"You look perfect," he assured her.

She batted her eyelash extensions at him. "Thanks."

Gilly decided to ignore this friendly exchange. "How's David?" she asked Royce.

"What's the matter with David?" Inge wanted to know.

"Somebody tried to mug him last night," Royce answered. "He got a nice crack on the head."

"Oh, the poor boy!" Inge exclaimed.

"Yes," said Gilly, grabbing her purse with its precious contents. "The poor boy."

They arrived at the van to find the others already there. Rob smiled at them and took Gilly's suitcase. "Thanks for hurrying," he said. "I want to make sure we get to take in Linderhof since we missed it the first time around."

"That will be great," said Gilly, not because she wanted to see the castle. The only tour she cared about taking was of the nearest Polizei station.

David came up beside her. "You haven't asked me how my head is," he complained.

Gilly knew she should pretend concern, but she was finding it increasingly difficult to talk to him. "I'm sorry," she said flatly. "How's your head?"

"It hurts," he snapped. "And I'd love to get my hands on the person who did it." With that he climbed into the back of the van next to Inge, who fussed over him and promised him he could lay his head on her shoulder.

"Lucky guy," said Clint, and Royce laughed.

Gilly ignored the comment (and the response) and climbed aboard.

They went through Oberammergau, home of the famous passion play, performed every ten years. The area was also famous for is wood carvings and Rob promised Lisa they'd back get there in time for her to buy one. But first he wanted to get them to the castle, which was nearby.

And beautiful. The area surrounding the castle looked like something from the pages of a fairy tale book. Gilly snapped a couple of shots out the window as they drove through the lush, green countryside.

"I'd like to come back here someday," she told Royce. "Rent a cottage and stay for about a year, maybe write the great American novel."

"You never told me you were a writer," he said.

"I'm not. But it would make a great excuse for doing something wild and crazy like that."

"Would you like to do something wild and crazy?"

"Maybe," she said, imitating his accent. "If I live that long," she added despondently.

He took her hand and squeezed it. "You will."

They proceeded down a small country road and wound up in a tree-lined parking lot which was already filling with cars and tour busses. A short walk along a wide, paved path brought them to a tourist area, complete with souvenir shops and snack stands.

Rob got in line to purchase their tickets to enter the castle and the famous grotto and the others went inside the attached gift shop to ogle its wares, "Lisa announcing that she was going to buy a cuckoo clock.

David parked himself on a bench, claiming his head hurt. "I'll wait here," he said. He looked up at Gilly. "Want to wait with me?"

If he thought she was going to be stupid enough to go anywhere alone with him or anyone, even if it was in a crowd, he was crazy. She declined his offer and, hugging her purse to her chest, followed the others into the shop.

She wanted to get something for her daughter, and she needed to replace the present she'd gotten for Janet.

The thought of the broken bottle of liqueur made her shiver. *Never mind that,* she told herself sternly, and purchased two dainty cups and saucers with a picture of the castle painted on them.

Royce joined her. "Hey, look at this," he said stepping over to a display of sterling silver souvenir charms. He pointed to a tiny carriage.

"Oh, cute!" Gilly touched the tiny charm and discovered that the little wheels moved.

"You got a charm bracelet?" he asked.

She shook her head regretfully. "No," she said.

"Well you should have. I'll take that Cinderella's carriage," he told the clerk.

Lisa came up behind them, holding the clock she'd just purchased. "What did you get?"

"Teacups for my daughter and my neighbor," answered Gilly. "And Prince Charming here is buying me a carriage."

Lisa grinned mischievously at Royce, then said, "Now you need to marry the prince and live happily ever after."

Royce grinned at Gilly and said, "I'm waitin' for her to let me see if the shoe fits," making her blush. He chuckled. "C'mon Cinderella. Let's go check out the castle."

David rejoined them once they came out, and from there they all went into the castle. He attached himself to her side and tried to snag her attention by whispered comments on everything they saw, but she ignored him and after a while, looking hurt, he drifted over to join Inge and Ed. Gilly watched him go with a sigh of relief and determined to enjoy the rest of the tour.

She was dazzled by the castle's opulence. Hard to believe this all was done for one man, she thought, gazing at the elaborately carved furniture and the priceless knick-knacks. She pointed to a huge crystal chandelier and whispered to Royce, "Buy me that."

"I already bought you a carriage. Don't be greedy."

Once they got back outside David turned up next to Gilly again like the proverbial bad penny, setting her nerves on edge once more.

"Let's plan to spend another hour looking around the grounds," Rob said to everyone. "Then we'll meet at the van and be on our way back to Oberammergau."

Where Gilly would march right to the police. One more hour, she told herself and clutched her purse tightly.

Rob consulted his watch. "The fountain in front of the castle should be going off in about half an hour. And don't forget to walk up to the grotto. Most people like that the best."

"That's where the little lake with the cockleboat is?" asked Lisa.

Rob nodded.

"Are you coming, too?" she asked.

He shook his head. "I've seen it several times."

With the exception of Ivan and Ida, who decided to rest by the fountain, everyone trooped off toward the grotto.

The mention of Oberammergau had wound Gilly's insides up tight and now all she could think about was getting to the police. But she decided her best chance of staying safe was to pretend she didn't know anything about anything.

Act normal, she told herself.

There was already a crowd waiting in front of the large, rock-shaped building, and it seemed to swallow their smaller group. Gilly began to fidget. Did she really want to be shut in a dark cave with both Carl and David? Or Ed and David? Anyone and David? Anyone and anyone? She looked at Royce, who stood unconcernedly chatting with Inge.

"I'm not sure I want to wait for the next tour," she announced. "There might not be time to see the fountain. Anybody want to go back?" *Royce?*

Just then the door opened and a man greeted them, first in German, then in English. The crowd surged forward, pushing her into the dark, dank cave.

Somewhere behind her she heard Ed. "I smell mold. It'll give me a headache. I'll see you all down at the fountain."

Good. Ed was now out of the picture and that meant being cooped up with one less possible murderer. And Royce was there to help her, she reminded herself.

As they entered the grotto she stole a look at David. He was totally absorbed with taking pictures so she allowed herself a moment to relax and admire the exquisite little lake, lighted by colored footlights. All around it hung cement stalactites. Anchored at the edge of the lake bobbed a little boat carved in the shape of a shell. Resisting the urge to jump the ropes cordoning off the lake and climb into it, she settled, instead, for taking a picture with her phone and hoped it would turn out.

She shot another glance David's direction. He was walking over to Inge, who was taking a selfie. Good. Feeling a little safer, Gilly wandered to the edge of the crowd, trying for an angle that would allow her to get a picture which included more of the lake.

Suddenly she felt something sharp prick her back. "Don't scream," commanded a hoarse whisper.

SIXTEEN

"What have you got in my back?" whispered Gilly.

"Don't play dumb," her captor hissed.

She looked over her shoulder and was shocked to see Rob. Rob!

"You wouldn't stab me in front of all these people," she told him. Except judging by the fact that his normal tolerant, long-suffering expression was long gone, replaced by something much darker, she had her doubts.

"I'd hate to," he admitted. He grabbed her arm in a vise-like grip and steered her further away from the crowd. "Let's go."

"I thought you didn't want to see the grotto."

"I don't." His grip got tighter and he picked up his pace.

Gilly cast a desperate glance in Royce's direction. He was busy taking pictures. Any minute he'd turn around and see Rob taking her away.

Or not. Inge latched onto his arm and got busy with her selfie stick. Great.

Feeling like a prisoner of war, she let Rob march her away from the crowd. Her mind was spinning; shock, anger and fear enjoying a free for all. So that was who she'd heard planning to take care of her back in Melk. She should never have assumed the voice she'd heard from her window was David's.

"And to think I thought you were so nice," she said bitterly.

"I'm sorry you had to get involved," he said, his soft, polite voice returning. "We're really not killers."

"Is that what you told the man you pushed off the Tegelberg?"

"What makes you think I had anything to do with that?" Rob hedged.

"His death couldn't have been a coincidence, not with all the other things that have happened on this trip. You had to be in on it. Now that I remember, you were missing when David made his big announcement. What was he supposed to be, a diversion of some kind?"

"You don't think I'd work with David, do you?" Rob, demanded, insulted. "I don't even like traveling with him."

"We found your books in his bucket bag."

"Just because I wouldn't work with him doesn't mean I wouldn't use him."

So Rob had been behind everything. Royce had been right, and she was the stupidest woman on the planet. Rob was the obvious choice for a criminal master mind. He was the one with all the time to do business while his flock chugged along the Rhine or enjoyed their free afternoons. And he had the van at his disposal for a late-night rendezvous. The note she'd found in her room at the castle in Oberwesel had been for him. He'd been expecting it. That was why he'd wanted her room.

"You know, really, leaving notes for each other in rooms – not very high tech."

"Not very traceable either after you burn them."

She thought of the man in the ice cream parlor. Maybe he'd been waiting to meet Rob. No wonder Rob had sent David packing. "You've had contacts everywhere, haven't you? What else have you been stealing?"

Rob didn't answer her.

"And poor Jan Van Yeck. You had him killed, didn't you?"

"You talk a lot, don't you?" Rob shot back.

"I guess so did Jan."

"Shut up," he snapped.

He hurried her along and the voice of the tour guide became only a distant echo. Gilly looked at the fake rock walls surrounding them. The Hall of the Mountain King, she thought grimly and shivered. Ahead of them she saw the exit, a door hidden in the mouth of the cave. "Now what?" she asked.

"We wait for your buddy Royce. By now I'm sure he's realized you're missing. He should come thundering along any minute."

"Yes, and with just a knife you won't be much of a match for him," Gilly sneered.

"Just a knife pointing in your back," Rob reminded her. "I think he'll do whatever I say."

"You might have a hard time explaining to the others why you're marching us around with a knife in my back."

"Oh, but I won't be with you for long. My partner will take care of you while I wait with the rest of the group. Of course, when you don't return, we'll report you missing. But..." He let the sentence trail off ominously.

"I suppose your partner has a gun," Gilly said.

"I suppose you're right," he agreed.

Gilly swallowed in a vain attempt to rehydrate her parched throat. Her eyes were having the opposite problem and she blinked in an effort to dam the tears.

It was all so wrong, so sad, so unfair. "This isn't the first time you've tried to take care of me, is it?"

"I never wanted to hurt you."

"I suppose it was your partner who pushed me into the street in Vienna."

"If you'd have just forgotten about those books. And then you had to go and make veiled threats in Krems, didn't you?"

"What are you talking about? I never threatened anyone."

"It's a moot point now."

Gilly glared at him. All along they'd thought David was the book thief. But it had been Rob. In Krems, right after the robbery at the abbey, Rob had been the last one down to the bar. He must have stayed behind to get his loot out of David's satchel and wrapped and addressed for mailing. Then in Augsburg, when they'd thought he was showering, he'd been rifling their rooms and stealing the books back. But how had they wound up back in David's bag?

"What were the books doing in David's bucket bag?" she demanded.

"I didn't realize you suspected any of us at first, and why you should have eventually settled on David of all people, God only knows," Rob said, his voice dripping with disdain. "I thought the books would be safe with him until I could find a minute away from all you parasites to get to the post office."

"How'd you sucker him into hauling them around for you, tell him you didn't have space in your luggage? And what was with the woman's name on the package?"

"Just a girlfriend back home."

"You mean an imaginary girlfriend."

Rob made no answer to that "I suppose he offered to carry the package until you could have a chance to mail it."

"I'd planned to in Augsburg, but you messed up that plan, you little pain in the ass.

Then we had that flat tire, and by the time we got to Landsberg the post office was closed."

"It serves you right. Didn't you ever hear the old saying about crime not paying?"

"It pays very well, believe me. And it will keep paying very well after I clean up this little mess."

"What are you going to do with us?" Gilly demanded. The question was an exercise in futility. She already knew the answer. Oooh, she was going to be sick.

"I'm sorry, Gilly," Rob said, his voice sounding strained. "But now I really need you to shut up."

She brazened it out and taunted, "Are you getting nervous? Afraid someone might hear us and come wreck all your plans?" She looked at the closed entrance. "How are you going to get out, anyway? Say abracadabra? When the tour guide and all those people come along I'll make a scene and with all those witnesses your knife won't help you."

"You forget I've done this tour a few times," he said. "I just have to flip a switch and we'll be out and on our way. But first I want my books."

"Your books?"

"Finders keepers."

"You and Ed will never get away with this."

"Ed!" Rob began to laugh.

"Ed isn't your partner?"

"You've got to be kidding."

That only left one possibility. Carl, strolling up the same path on the Tegelberg that the hysterical David had used only minutes before, encouraging Rob to leave the abbey before the theft could be discovered, making veiled threats to her in the hotel in Krems. Good old, German speaking, disapproving Carl.

"It's Carl, isn't it?" she demanded.

"The books, Gilly."

She jutted out her jaw. "No."

"The books," he snarled.

The knife poked through Gilly's top and she felt sudden pain. She yelped and dropped her sack containing the teacups and charm Royce had bought her. The sound of a muffled crunch told her their fate.

"That's the second time you've made me break something," she stormed. Something took over – rage, idiocy, PMS. Without thinking, she whirled around, swinging her purse like a broad sword and whacked Rob on the side of the head.

Thrown off balance, he staggered back against the wall just as Royce rounded the corner. Without slowing down, he was on Rob, driving his fist into Rob's jaw and sending him sliding down the wall, unconscious.

The danger over, reaction set in and Gilly's whole body began to shake.

Royce shoved Rob to one side. He pointed a finger at him and turned to Gilly. "There! Didn't I tell you it was him?"

"Well, if you knew it was him why weren't you watching him?" she retorted.

"Sorry. I thought he'd gone off somewhere to wait for us. I guess that's what we were supposed to think."

Gilly pressed her lips together and hugged herself.

Belatedly, Royce wrapped his arms around her and asked her if she was alright.

"Yeah, and thanks for saving me."

"You looked like you were doin' fine on your own, actually."

"Neither one of us will be doing fine unless we get away from here," she said, thinking of Rob's silent partner.

"It's okay," said Royce. "He's out cold."

"He's got a partner, with a gun. We've got to get out of here!" Gilly could hear the hysteria in her voice. Looking at the mysteriously shut door intensified the feeling.

"Okay." Royce moved to the door and pushed against it, but it refused to move. He glared at it and swore.

"There's a switch or something that triggers it," said Gilly. "Rob told me."

"Did he say where it was?"

She shook her head. Her eyes fell on a small metal door set in the wall to the right of the exit. "What's that?"

"Good job! That's gotta be it. And goin' out this way will be a lot quicker than fightin' the crowd back there." He pulled open the little metal door and fiddled with a switch. Lights came on.

"Just what we need," Gilly said irritably. Even though he was unconscious, Rob's near proximity had her on the edge of hyperventilation. Knowing he had someone lying in wait for them somewhere nearby didn't do much for her nerves, either.

"Hey, tryin' here," Royce snapped.

"Sorry," she muttered. "Try that one," she said, pointing to another switch.

Seconds dragged by while they fiddled with switches and levers. At last they heard a click.

"That's it!" He pushed the door open and they dashed from the cave.

"Be careful," Gilly cautioned. "Carl's probably lurking out there in the bushes somewhere right now."

"Carl?" Royce came to a sudden stop.

"Yes, Carl." She pushed him back into motion. "Rob was going to deliver us to him and I have no idea where."

"How do you know it's Carl?"

"Because Rob as much as told me. We'll have to warn the others and find someone to take us to the police."

They galloped down the path from the grotto, then crossed the castle grounds in record time, heading for the wide cement path that led to the parking lot. Gilly was getting winded and her side hurt. To make matters worse, she remembered she'd left the little charm Royce had bought her laying on the floor of the grotto, along with her broken cups, but she ran doggedly on, dodging tourists as she went.

Panting and wheezing, they reached the parking lot and jogged up to the van. It was open and Ivan and Ida were already there. Ida sat in a back seat, her shoes off, while her husband lounged in front on the driver's side, napping with his head on the steering wheel.

A look of concern spread over her face at the sight of them. "Gilly! What on earth...?"

Gilly didn't let her finish. "We've got to get to the nearest police station," she said as she scrambled into the back of the van. Now!" She took in the fact that the van was unlocked. "Did Rob give you the keys to the van?" There was a lucky break.

"Yes," said Ida. Mr. Thompson's feet hurt."

"Thank God for Ivan's sore feet," Gilly said as Royce climbed into the front passenger seat and pulled the door shut.

"Never mind his feet. What's going on?" Ida demanded. "Ivan, wake up," she snapped. "Something's wrong."

Ivan snorted awake and lifted his head.

"We'll explain on the way," Gilly said. "Start driving, Ivan."

"Mr. Thompson doesn't have a license to drive in Europe," said Ida. "We need to wait for Rob."

"That's the last thing we want to do," said Royce. "Come on, Ivan. Get this thing movin'. This is an emergency."

Ivan looked to his wife, then shrugged and started the engine.

"Where's Rob?" Ida demanded.

"He's in the grotto, unconscious," Gilly replied.

Ida gasped. "Unconscious! We don't need the police. We need a doctor."

"Trust me," Gilly told her. "We need the police. Rob isn't what he appears to be. He's a thief. Head for Oberammergau," she ordered Ivan. "I saw signs for it when we passed through earlier."

They drove in tense silence for a few minutes. Then a puzzled expression settled on Royce's face. "Wait a minute, he said. "Oberammergau is that way..."

Ivan reached into his shirt, and just as Royce turned toward him, pulled out a gun and pointed it at Royce. "Sit still, country boy."

Gilly's mouth flew open.

"Hell," muttered Royce. "Who'd a thought it?"

"Oh, Ida. Not you," Gilly said in disappointment.

"I'm sorry, dear," Ida said. "You've continued to be a problem and now look what you've done."

"What *I've* done? What about all the things you've done?"

"I'm afraid it wasn't very friendly of you to insinuate I was lying back at the monastery, dear" Ida replied. "What could I think but that... well, never mind."

"That I'd seen you." And, ironically, she had. Getting away with those books, which Ida had probably slipped in that big purse of hers. All Gilly had focused on was the bucket bag.

"And once you began interfering you really complicated matters. Oh, yes, you certainly kept us on our toes."

So that was why Rob had thought it would be safer to have David carrying the books. He'd thought Gilly suspected his partner. Sweet, harmless, everyone's mom, Ida Thompson.

"You could get us into a lot of trouble and we can't have that."

"This trip wasn't a good one," Ivan muttered.

"You've done this before?" Gilly stammered.

"A few times," Ida said modestly.

"How are you going to explain our absence to the rest of the group?" taunted Royce.

"That will be easy," Ida said. "You two decided to leave us and get married. Rob took you into ... Schwangau," she decided, naming a town in the opposite direction.

"Rob is unconscious in the grotto," Gilly reminded her.

"Oh yes, that's right," said Ida. "Thanks to you," she added, narrowing her eyes at Gilly. "We'll have to think of something else, won't we Mr. Thompson?"

"I suppose so," her husband said.

"I can't believe this is happening," cried Gilly. "Ida, why? How could you let Rob lure you into such a thing?"

Ivan chuckled. "Like mother like son."

Gilly blinked. "Rob is your son?" Now she could see the resemblance – the round face and snub nose, the similar coloring. "But you don't have the same last name," she protested.

"Oh, Rob is my stepson," put in Ivan, sounding as proud as if he'd been Rob's natural father.

"So there's a whole gang of you," Gilly said in disgust. "And you use this tour group thing as a cover." She shook her head. "That's great. Rob is the guide and you two are just a sweet, retired couple who steal and kill people for a hobby."

Gilly's last words made Ida scowl. "And I thought you were such a nice, young woman. Looks are sure deceiving."

You could say that again. "Who pushed that poor man off the Tegelberg?" Gilly demanded.

"Rob," Ivan said quickly. Paternal pride obviously didn't extend to taking the rap for something his stepson did. "Actually, I'm afraid we were having a disagreement. The man felt we were going to double-cross him..."

"That will be enough, Mr. Thompson," said his wife, and Ivan fell silent.

Double-cross. "How do you say double-cross in German?" asked Gilly.

"You figured out the note at the castle, didn't you?" guessed Ivan.

"Mr. Thompson!" snapped Ida.

"Sorry," he said, telling Gilly who'd taken the note from her purse. Ida had visited her room in the castle in Oberwesel. While Gilly had been in the bathroom, Ida had been getting rid of incriminating evidence, stuffing the note in that nubby yellow sweater of hers.

The pieces of the puzzle were falling into place to make a very ugly picture. Poor Van Yeck, with his rich contacts, had been involved with Rob and his gang. In his drunken state that night at the Hotel Triannon, he must have somehow let it slip to Rob that he'd been bragging about their business dealings, and his loose lips had earned him an "accidental" death. The Dutch gangster hadn't stumbled into David's room in Amsterdam by mistake. He had, most likely, already killed Van Yeck and come to collect his blood money from Rob. The villains they'd seen along the way had all probably been part of an enormous web of second rate criminals.

"What else do you steal?" Gilly demanded. "It can't be that easy in most places."

"We find ways of picking up ... souvenirs here and there," Ida said complacently. "We have friends all over Europe and those friends have friends, and access to ..." She stopped, frowned, and then clamped her lips shut.

"So you don't just rob museums. You rob private homes, too."

"I think we've chatted enough," Ida said. From her tone of voice one might have thought she was simply tired of talking about the weather.

"This is horrible," Gilly whimpered. "All those people..."

"If you weren't such a nosy busybody you'd never have noticed," Ida said.

Gilly remembered their evening in Landsberg. Ivan and Ida had been unusually sociable that night, staying with them in the restaurant. Until she and Royce had followed David and his satchel containing their valuable package. They hadn't been being sociable. They'd been protecting their interests. So much for following Gilly because they were concerned about her.

Why hadn't she seen that? She'd suspected everyone else. Probably the only thing that had saved her and Royce from getting their throats slit that evening had been the appearance of Clint and Lisa.

What would save them now?

Ida fired something at Ivan in German. He nodded and began to slow down.

Looking for a place to bump them off, Gilly realized. She looked at Royce in panic. "Do something!"

"What do you want me to do?" he retorted. "He's got a gun."

"Which he's going to use any minute," Gilly reminded him, her voice rising.

Royce still did nothing.

I have a daughter to finish raising. I don't want to die, Gilly thought. *Not now, not when I've been just beginning to live!* She looked at Royce, who was looking at Ivan, then, with a frustrated squeal, thrust herself over the seat and tried for the gun.

Ida grabbed her and Royce dove for Ivan. The van swerved and the gun went off, turning Gilly deaf and sending a bullet zinging out the open window.

Ida hooked an arm around Gilly's waist and began pulling her back onto the seat. With superhuman effort, Gilly lunged over Ivan's left shoulder and caught hold of the steering wheel and the van swerved again.

Ida caught a handful of Gilly's hair and yanked and, with a shriek, Gilly fell backwards. The darned woman was stronger than she looked.

As she fought with Ida the two men continued to struggle, turning the steering wheel in the process, and careening the van off the road and into a ditch. Even with Ivan's foot no longer on the gas the van had enough momentum to bump and skid like an amusement park ride and suddenly nobody was fighting with anybody.

The ride ended when it tipped on its side, tossing its passengers every which way. *Buckle up. It's the law. Oops.*

Everything went black for Gilly, not because she lost consciousness but because Ida fell on top of her face. After several muffled cries, the weight of Ida came off her and she struggled up to see Royce, holding the dazed woman by her blouse collar. Ivan lay slumped sideways in the front seat, unconscious.

Royce clambered out of the van and after several grunts and much swearing, managed to get the door open. Then he helped Gilly climb out.

Her legs wobbled under her when she landed and she sat down suddenly. "Sorry," she mumbled.

"You okay? Anything broken?"

"I don't think so, but everything sure hurts."

He held out a hand and pulled her to her feet. "Hang in there. It's almost over."

"Help me," Ida called weakly.

"Don't worry. We ain't leavin' you behind," Royce growled, and hauled her from the van.

Inside, Ivan was still inert. "Do you think he's okay?" Gilly asked.

"Do you care? Come on, let's go," said Royce. He turned to Ida, showing her Ivan's gun. "You too, Baby Doll."

They set off down the road, Ida moaning and stumbling between them.

"Do you think we should have tied Ivan up?" Gilly fretted.

"I don't think he's going anywhere for a while," said Royce. Once he wakes up, he'll never get that van out of the ditch, and he's in no condition to walk very far."

"I'm not walking all the way to the next town," Ida informed them. "I'm hurt."

Gilly glared at her. "Boo-hoo," she said, and then to Royce, "It's going to be a long, hard walk. Maybe we'd better try to get a ride."

They tried to hitch a ride from the next three cars that zipped past. "Why don'tcha yank up your skirt and show 'em some leg," Royce suggested. "That'll get somebody to stop."

"The last two cars to come by have been driven by women, smart guy," Gilly shot back. "If you want to get us a ride into town peel off your shirt."

"Hey, I ain't embarrassed to be a sex object for a good cause," he said, and undid his shirt.

The next person was a Generation Z German in a low-slung sports car, who merely honked and waved at them as he sped by.

In spite of the seriousness of their situation, Gilly laughed. This brought a scowl from Royce. "Sorry," she said. "It must be nerves. Maybe you should just run out in front of somebody and hold out your hand. Then they'd have to stop."

"The way these guys drive? I'd be a pancake."

Gilly sighed, all the laughter drained out of her.

Ida groaned. "I can't go any further."

"Well, we ain't gonna sit here and wait for your boyfriend to come give us a lift," Royce said, starting her in motion again.

They hadn't gone too far when a middle-aged man in a

Volvo pulled up next to them. "Möchten Sie mitfahren?" he called.

"Bitte?" asked Gilly.

"He leaned over and opened the passenger door. "Mit-fahren," he repeated, gesturing them in.

"A ride! Oh, yes. Ja, danke," she said, and they climbed in.

"Do you think you can tell this guy to get us to the police?" Royce asked her.

"I'll try," said Gilly. She stuttered out their destination and the reason for it as best she could, hoping the good Samaritan would understand her.

The man's eyes widened and his foot pressed down on the accelerator.

"What'd you tell him?" asked Royce.

"I know I told him we needed to get to the police. And I hope I told him a man is dead. I'm not sure, but I think I might have threatened to kill him, instead."

"Either way, it'll get us to the cops," said Royce.

TWO HOURS later they were still sitting in the police station along with the rest of their group who'd all been rounded up, waiting for the police to finish sorting everything out, trying to find answers themselves.

"Poor David," Gilly said and moved the ice pack she'd been given from her shoulder to her knee. "I feel guilty for even suspecting him. I'll have to find some way to make this up to him."

Royce studied David, who sat across from them, talking animatedly to Lisa. "I think you've already done a lot for him. You've given him enough adventures to be the life of everyone's party for the next ten years." He shook his head. "You know, the kid was lucky. He'd'a been finished if we'd made it to the police with these books. Nobody'd have believed his story about holding them for Rob to mail."

"You were right after all. He was the fall guy." Gilly shook her head. "As busy as he was with everybody's business, I'm surprised he didn't talk to Rob about mailing his package in front of all of us."

"Just dumb luck," said Royce. "Pretty stupid risk on Rob's part, if you ask me."

"Oh, I don't know," said Gilly. "It's like hiding something in plain sight. People overlook it because they're searching in all the hard places. No one would have guessed that the package was the stolen books, anyway, probably not even us. What else do you think they were into?" she asked.

Royce shook his head. "Beats me. They knew enough people to be into plenty of stuff. There probably ain't a tourist attraction in Europe they haven't looted. Then there were all those contacts they had passing them stuff." He rubbed the back of his neck. "Shit. What a weird thing to stumble into. And poor old Ed. He looked so danged insulted when he found out you suspected him of bein' a master criminal."

She still suspected him of snitching diamonds but after everything they'd been through no way was she going there.

"You didn't need to tell him that, you know." She looked at Ed, sitting on the same bench as David and Lisa, Inge asleep on his shoulder. He gave her an embarrassed smile. "It was an easy enough mistake, "she said. "He sure behaved like a criminal in that diamond cutter's in Amsterdam. And then there was that little talk he gave me in the elevator."

"Yeah," Royce agreed. "I gotta admit I'd probably have jumped to the same conclusion myself."

"I guess I jumped to conclusions about Carl, too," Gilly said with a sigh.

Royce gave her hand a squeeze. "That's okay. He made a good candidate."

"He did happen to be in the right place at the right time up there on the Tegelberg," she said.

"Yeah, and don't forget that list of contacts," put in Royce, trying to look serious. He failed and began to snicker.

"Go ahead, laugh. How was I to know it was a list of prospective brides?"

"Inge knew," said Royce.

"Humph," said Gilly.

"You know, it's funny," he said. "When you don't have all the answers you either miss clues or see them all wrong."

"Like what?"

"Like some of the things Ida said to Rob. Who'd talk to a grown man like that except his mother?"

"Boy, you're right there. That comment she made when David got sick in the van certainly had a double meaning when you look at it in light of the conversation I overheard in Krems. How I could have mistaken Rob's voice for David's I'll never know."

"Easy. You thought David was in the room next to you. People see and hear what they expect to see and hear. And remember how you saw Ida pick up David's bag before we all went into the library at the abbey?" Royce continued. "It was her you almost caught heading out the door, but you associated that bag with David and just assumed it was him."

"He had it when I saw him again."

Royce nodded. "I saw Ida give it to him when we went outside. Just the group's mom, pickin' up after one of us. Gotta hand it to her. That little stunt took nerve."

Gilly shook her head. "I guess we should have compared notes a little better."

"We'll do better next time," said Royce.

She looked at him incredulously. "Next time?"

He grinned. "Of course. The rest of this trip's a bust. We'll have to take another."

Gilly smiled, appreciating his logic. "You're right," she said.

"Maybe bring along your kid, if she likes me."

"Who wouldn't?"

He smiled at that, then put an arm on her shoulder, snuggling her up against him. "So, where you wanna go? Italy, Switzerland?"

Gilly turned thoughtful. "You know, she said, "it might be fun to take one of those mystery cruises."

Made in the USA
Middletown, DE
16 June 2024

55895767R00110